Whatever He Wants

Whatever He Wants
M. St. Goar

New Tradition Books

Whatever He Wants
by
M. St. Goar

New Tradition Books
ISBN 1932420835

For information contact:
New Tradition Books
newtraditionbooks@yahoo.com

For all the people who think they missed the boat.
And Lil' E.

1

When you see the way I dress, I know your first impression is that I'm looking to get fucked. And you're right. I am looking to get fucked. I want to be fucked all the time. My switch has been flipped and I'm ready for action. I crave sex with strangers. I love fucking both men and women. I love sucking cock and I get wet just thinking about all the sexual possiblities there are in the world. My boyfriend, Paul, fucks the daylights out of me, better than anyone, but sometimes this is still not enough. Sometimes, even his big cock is not enough to satisfy me. When it's not, I do whatever he tells me to do. I trust him with my sexual satisfaction. I fuck whoever he says to fuck and do whatever crazy thing he imagines. And the funny thing about it is that I'm still not even sure if I'm a slut. As far as I'm concerned, I'm just a girl who likes to have sex. A lot. And Paul makes sure that I'm always happy. He has control of me and I feel better than I ever did in my life before I met him. And you know something? I don't care what you think about it. I am who I am and you just have to live with it.

Okay, I know this is a little sordid for most of the normal world to understand but really it all started quite innocently. Actually it was a blind date that got the ball rolling.

I had recently gotten divorced and was still a little raw when my friend at work, Doreen, suggested that I go out with him. At the time, I was doing my best to try to live the fabulous life of the newly single but was doing a rather pitiful job at it. The rush that you get from mimosas and Sunday brunch can only sustain you for so long before it just becomes yet another routine like going to work or doing laundry. I had gotten married young and had spent all of my adult life with one man. As a result of this, I felt a little bit stunted relationship-wise, but was still a little at odds at how to get started. Add the fact that I was trying to assert myself as an independent woman and you can see just what a mess I was. I was thankful that was only in my late-twenties and had the "rest of my life" ahead of me so to speak. Regardless, I was doing everything in the world to show that I didn't need a man and that I was okay on my own. However, mostly my independence meant sitting at home every night in my one bedroom apartment drinking wine and eating lean cuisines while watching reality dating shows. I also worked out a lot because I was so "independent" that I didn't have much else to do. At least I had that. I didn't let myself completely go the way a lot of women in similar circumstances do.

Now, let me preface this part by saying that Doreen is a little on the wild side. She's a free spirit who never really seems to care what other people think about her. She had even gotten a boob job much to the chagrin of all the other women in the office.

Earlier, before she had had one, I had actually said that I was thinking about getting a reduction. She looked at me like I was crazy. "I would love to have what you have! Are you kidding? Natural double D's!"

"But they're so heavy!" I had said. "And men can't keep their eyes off them! It makes me feel like I'm on display all the time."

She rolled her eyes. "I would love it if men stared at my boobs the way they do yours."

"Really?" I replied. I was so naïve then. Now, I cringed at how I stupid I was. I just didn't get it. I had been given these great gifts and had hidden and been ashamed of them. Now, I love to show them off. They make it so much easier to convey what I'm about and what I like to do. It's so odd that women who are born with big breasts are always embarrassed by them and want them reduced and women who have small breasts always want bigger ones. But then again, low self esteem comes in all shapes and forms. If women would just accept the fact that most men are turned on by the very fact that they are women, the world would be a much sexier place.

However, even after she told me this, it took me a while to really start accepting what nature had so generously given me. But eventually, I began to understand what she was saying and started appreciating them a little more. Even so, it wasn't until Paul came along though that I really started showing them off and being proud of them. Doreen was a big help in changing my perspective about them though. After she got the boob job, I knew exactly what she was talking about. I saw how men looked at her and even felt a little envious that she could be so confident with herself.

I wanted to be more like her. I wanted to be the sort of woman who works it. And after my divorce from my college sweetheart had devastated me, I needed anything that would help me get back my confidence. I wanted to get back in the game and see what else was out there. I felt that I deserved to have a good time, just like the one that everyone else seemed to be having. So I accepted her invitation to the blind date. I figured that anyone who was friends with her must be fun. Besides, I wasn't doing anything else except laundry.

. . . .

The plan was for Paul (who at that time I was still referring to as "The Mystery Man) and I to meet Doreen and her husband, Tom, at a concert in the park on Friday night. It was the summer concert series. Doreen said that this would make things less uncomfortable for everyone. Especially her husband. He hated doing this kind of stuff, she said.

And that's what we did. The park was near my apartment so I could walk to it easily. I arrived early and sat on one of the benches in the part of the park that Doreen had prearranged as the place to meet and waited for someone to show up. Fortunately, it was Doreen and her husband. I wouldn't have to handle the initial awkwardness of talking to my blind date by myself. The band wasn't supposed to start for another hour. Besides, I probably wouldn't have even known who the Mystery Man was. That would have made an awkward situation even more uncomfortable.

"You look great," Doreen said.

"Thanks," I said, not that convinced. I was just wearing a skirt and top that I had had for a while but had never really had the opportunity to wear. I was still far from being confident about myself at that time.

"You look great too," I said. And she did. She of course was flaunting her new cleavage, but still looked classy.

"I'll say she does. Great rack too. I really got my money's worth." Tom said laughing.

Doreen blushed, but I knew she loved it. I really envied their relationship.

"So, when is he supposed to be here?" I asked.

Tom looked at his watch. "Paul should be here anytime. He said that he had a couple of things to do before he got here, but would do his best not to be late."

It turns out that Paul worked in the same office building as Tom. They had had a friendly acquaintance for several years. After Doreen was by chance introduced to him when she had gone to see Tom at work one day, she had pressed her husband for details about him. After finding out that he was single and appeared to be quite wealthy, she had forced Tom to set up a double date. That Doreen was such a character.

"And he's European. How romantic is that?"

I couldn't help but laugh and roll my eyes.

A few minutes later, he finally showed up. When I first saw him from a distance, I didn't figure that there was any way that this could be the guy. He was very well dressed—but casually of course and very good looking. He was probably in his early to mid-thirties, had almost black hair and was in very good shape. He was also tall. There was no way a guy like this was not taken. And moreover there was no way that a guy like this would ever go on a blind date. He wouldn't need to. He probably had women throwing themselves at him. But when he walked over and said hello and shook Tom's hand, I knew that I was wrong. This was the guy. Even if he turned out to be a complete asshole, at least I would have something nice to look at for the rest of the evening.

"This is Paul," Tom said. "He works in the building with me."

"And this is Elise," Doreen said hurriedly.

Paul looked at me and smiled. He seemed a little reserved but regardless seemed to be very sure of himself. Like a guy who knows he's very good looking but doesn't like people to make a big deal of it. I liked that.

5

After the introductions, Doreen suggested that we go over one of the nearby bars and have some cocktails before the concert. We were all happy to go because everyone knows there's nothing like a little alcohol to get the conversation going.

Once we had had a couple of drinks, everyone loosened up and started talking. Paul was still relatively quiet, but I could tell that he was enjoying himself. I told him that I was recently divorced. He said that he had been a long term relationship, but it had ended badly. All in all, it was just fairly common smalltalk. We didn't really pair up or anything. Just talked across the table.

Even though Doreen had said that he was European, I was having a hard time believing this. He barely had any sort of accent at all. He could have been from the Midwest for all I could figure. I had to ask.

"Paul, Doreen says that you're from Europe?"

"Yes, I'm from Belgium. I'm Flemish," he said smiling. I couldn't help but notice that he had perfect teeth. And when he had said Belgium, his accent had finally become barely detectable.

"But you don't have an accent."

"I actually grew up in the Netherlands so we watched a lot of American television. It's how we practiced our English. I personally was addicted to the A-Team."

"But you speak English so well."

"Maybe we should make watching television a requirement in our schools," Tom laughed.

"It would probably help," Paul said being completely serious, but then he started laughing too. "Especially the A-Team."

After a little while, we could hear that the concert had started up.

"Well, let's go back over there. That's why we're here after all," Doreen said laughing.

We paid our tab and walked over to the concert. As usual, it was some sort of jazz fusion band that was neither boring or edgy enough to offend any of the people who financed these summer concert events. We sat there and listened and drank some more cocktails. This was when Doreen and Tom apparently decided that Paul and I should pair off. They had subtley walked to a short distance away when they had gone to get drinks. They then began having a conversation with another couple. I hadn't even noticed that they had even left. This gave Paul and I a little time to talk even though I didn't really know what to say.

"Tom's a great guy, isn't he?" I said.

"Yes, he is," Paul said over the music. "I don't really know him that well, but he's always been nice to me."

We stood in silence there for a while.

"So what do you do?" I asked. "I'm in advertising."

"I'm in banking," he said and smiled. "It's very boring and, unless you're interested in the minute details of international currency exchange, I won't bother you with the details."

"Thanks," I said honestly because stuff like that really hurt my head.

We exchanged more small talk like that for the rest of the concert and when it was over, Tom and Doreen finally came back over to us.

"So did you two hit it off?" Doreen asked, a little drunk.

"Doreen!" Tom said.

"Oh, it's okay," Paul said. "I think we hit it off nicely, don't you think, Elise?"

I was a little surprised and secretly a little glad. "Sure," I said.

"Well, I need to pour this one into bed," Tom said facetiously. Doreen fake punched him in the shoulder and laughed.

We said our goodbyes but before I could leave, Paul stopped me.

"Doreen said that you live near here. I could walk you home, if you don't mind."

"I would like that," I said, truthfully. I really liked him and the fact that he seemed to like me made him even more attractive.

We started towards my apartment, not saying anything. Normally such silences would make me uncomfortable but it was different with Paul. I could tell that his silence wasn't because he didn't know what to say, but rather because he didn't want to talk all over the mood.

We walked down a couple of streets and were nearing my building when we heard something in an alley nearby. It sounded to me like someone was being attacked. There was moaning and groaning and yelling. We walked over to see more clearly and saw that my initial impression was wrong. It was a couple having sex on the hood of a car. Right there where everyone could see them. And they didn't seem to care one bit who watched. The girl was sitting on top of the guy, riding him like there was no tomorrow. The top of her strapless dress was down around her stomach, exposing her large breasts and her skirt was up around her waist. The guy still had his shirt on but his pants were around his ankles. They both looked a little drunk but not so much that they were unattractive. She was really grinding on him and he was loving ever second of it. At one point, the woman looked around at me, smiled and just kept riding. It was as if she was saying that she knew that I would love to be her right then. She began riding him even harder and had an orgasm right there in front of us. This didn't stop them though because they just kept going. It was one of the most erotic things I had ever seen.

"Well, I guess they certainly enjoyed the concert," Paul said, smiling and trying hard not to laugh.

I didn't really know what to say. My face was flushed from the embarrassment of seeing something so private. I wanted to feign disgust because that's how I had been brought up, but I really didn't feel that way. Actually I was intrigued and the fact that these two were having sex in public like this with pure abandon was turning me on. I could almost feel my mouth watering just thinking about how they were going at it. I had always loved sex and sexual things but had kept this to myself. I had grown up in a very strict home where girls were taught not to do anything that might be considered slutty. But I had always had a desire to see this kind of thing. Loose women and prostitutes fascinated me and I was in awe of women who had sex just for fun. However, I never expressed this to anyone because of my upbringing. My ex-husband only had a faint idea of how dirty my fantasies were. Even though we had some pretty hot sex at times, he had actually considered me to be a little on the prudish side. This was how tightly I kept my sexual thoughts to myself. He had no idea how much I masturbated to my fantasies while we were married.

"I suppose so," I replied.

Sensing that I was a little uncomfotable, Paul suggested that we move on. "We don't want them to think we're perverts do we?"

"Certainly not," I said a little bit too emphatically.

Paul looked at me a little curiously. I could almost tell that he knew that I was putting on. That I wanted to stay and watch but he didn't say anything and his face was inscrutable. However, if I didn't know any better, I would have almost thought his eyes were smiling at me.

He walked me to the door of my building. I wasn't sure whether to kiss him or not, so I didn't. I didn't want to do anything I would regret so I just shook his hand. I didn't want to give him the wrong idea especially after what we had just seen in the alley. He smiled and asked if he could call me again. I said yes and gave him my number. I was glad that he asked.

We said our goodbyes and I went upstairs.

As I lay in bed that night, I couldn't get the thought of the couple having sex on the car out of my head. I got out of bed and took my vibrator from my nightstand. It was the first time I had turned it on since my divorce. I stepped out of my clothes and started rubbing my breasts. While I had been a little ashamed of them in public, in private they had always been a great pleasure to me. I loved caressing my nipples. I kept thinking about the woman on the car. I imagined that I was her. That I was fucking a man in full view of whoever wanted to see. I thought about how wonderful it would be to have my breasts out for the whole world to look at. No embarrassment. I imagined people masturbating to me while I orgasmed. I got more and more turned on from these fantasies. From there I moved to the bed and lay down. I put the vibrator against my pussy. It felt so good. The pleasure from the vibration was enough to almost put my fantasies out of my head. It was going to be a huge orgasm and I could feel that it was getting closer. My body tingled. I was so horny I couldn't stand it. I rubbed my breasts as I touched the vibrator to my clit. I hadn't had any form of sex since I had divorced and this felt beyond good. It felt so wonderful to be sexual again. Even if it was in my bedroom with a vibrator. It had never let me down before and I knew it wouldn't this time. As I put in the vibrator I couldn't help but take my other hand and rub my clit. I remembered the girl on the car again and thought about her full breasts going up and down as she ground against that guy. I thought about how his penis must have felt in her, thrusting up into her vagina. I rubbed my wet clit some more and brought my hand up to my mouth and tasted myself. This had always been one of my secret pleasures. I loved the taste of myself and the thought of what I was doing brought me that much closer to coming. I thought about the woman on the car and the look on her face when she orgasmed. I thought about the look in the man's face as he strained to keep from coming.

Then it was there. The orgasm was huge and my body shuddered as I came. I couldn't help moaning out loud from the spasms. It felt great and it seemed to go on forever. But as soon as it was over, I couldn't help but go for another. This one came more quickly. My body almost convulsed with the sensation and the release that that the vibrator gave me. Again, I could just imagine myself as the woman who was on top of the guy. The way she rode him, with her breasts showing for the whole world to see. The way she looked at me and smiled. I did want to be her so badly. To be like her and so free. I couldn't stop masturbating and I kept orgasming until I was exhausted. I soon fell asleep and slept better than I had in months.

2

Of course, it wasn't that long after that I fucked him. That we had sex, rather.

After the concert, I couldn't get him out of my mind. I had had a great time talking to him and he was just so handsome and nice. I was very happy when he called the next day to ask me out. While I had never done this kind of thing before, I had already decided that if things went right and he wasn't a creep or a psycho, I was going to have sex with him. After all, I had only been with one man in my life, so it wasn't like I had the habit of picking up random guys. I was just ready for a little adventure. I didn't know if it was him or seeing the couple on the hood of the car, but after that blind date, I couldn't get the idea of sex out of my mind. In fact, I found myself masturbating frequently again, just as I had when I was married. I felt alive again. It was so good for my fantasies to return.

He said that he would pick me up on Sunday morning. I was happy that he had called. It would be so nice to be going out on Sunday morning with a guy for a change.

I had thought that decorum dictated that this was a little too soon after the initial date to go out, but I was pleased that I wouldn't have to wait to see him again. He seemed pleased that I accepted as well. He said that the reason, other than the fact that he wanted to see me again, was that he was going out of town on business for a couple of weeks. He said that he couldn't wait that long to see me again. I thought that it was so sweet that he had said this. Also, I was relieved that he wasn't playing any games with me. That was always one of the biggest things I had dreaded about starting to date. The games. I was too straightforward of a person for them. When I liked someone, I liked them. It was hard for me to pretend otherwise.

Sunday rolled around and he picked me up. He drove a Mercedes of course. I shouldn't have been surprised. Doreen had said that he was loaded, but I thought that she was probably exaggerating just to try to sell me on the idea of the date.

We went to the restaurant and had brunch. We small talked some more, but I think both of us sensed what was next. We knew that we would soon be having sex. The chemistry between us was almost palpable. At least I hoped that's what my women's intuition was telling me. It had been so long since I had even anticipated having sex that it could have been cloudy. I was so horny I could have been seeing signs that weren't there. My libido had been greatly diminished during my marriage simply due to the same problems that affect most married women's sex drives. The very fact that they can get fucked anytime they want greatly diminishes their desire to do so.

It wasn't like that now. There was some uncertainty here. And this only made me want to get fucked even more. It made me want to make it happen. And he just looked so good, with his black hair and slightly tanned skin. I could already feel my arms around his broad back and shoulders. I crossed and uncrossed my legs in anticipation. I was really beginning to get wet.

I had nothing to fear as far as what would happen next though. Without saying anything too direct about having sex, we both hurried up and ate. We also had champagne of course because after all it was brunch.

"Would you like to go somewhere else?" he asked as we walked back to his car. I could tell that he already knew where we were going.

"I don't know. Do you have any ideas?" I was still too ladylike at this point to come out and tell him that I wanted to wrap my legs around him and fuck the daylights out of him.

He thought for a minute, as if trying to figure out a tactful way of asking me back to his place. I could tell he wasn't the kind of guy who did this kind of thing, being so spontaneous. Like most Europeans I've met, he was actually rather formal in the way he acted. I know, as Americans, we always see the wild and crazy ones on TV, the ones who are always telling us how uptight and repressed we are. But in real life, I had only met a few of those. Most of them were actually rather very stodgy. I didn't think he was stodgy at all, but just a little reserved. Unlike some people, it worked with him. It actually added to his attractiveness.

"Would you like to come back to my apartment and drink more champagne?" he asked, smiling.

"I think that's a great idea," I said as my breathing began to quicken in anticipation.

. . . .

We had barely gotten into his apartment before we started in at each other. We both hungered for each other's bodies and I couldn't wait to get out of my clothes. I couldn't wait to get him out of his either. All those months of sexual deprivation were pent up and waiting to be unleashed. I was only glad that I had such a hunk of a guy to unleash them upon. I wanted him to grope me all over. I wanted to put my hands all over him. Our lips met and it was like we were both on fire. He kissed me deeply and I put his hands upon my breasts. My nipples were already hard as he careessed them and pulled off my top. I unsnapped my bra because I wanted him to suck my nipples so badly. When his mouth met them, I gasped. His mouth barely covered just part of my breasts but it was enough. Just seeing him sucking them and getting so turned on by them made me so wet I couldn't stand it. His hands went to my ass and I couldn't help but grind against his leg, rubbing my pussy against his thigh. I could feel his cock hardening as I rubbed against him. I would have to be fucked soon, but I didn't want to get ahead of myself and miss out on any of the good foreplay that was sure to come.

My hand went to his cock which was now fully hard. Even though he still had on his pants, I could feel that it was big. I was glad. A guy that good looking without a big cock would have been a tragedy. He took off his shirt and I could finally see just a great body he had. His muscles were big but not bulky. They were defined and hard. I couldn't wait to get my hands on his chest and ass. I wanted his arms around me and squeezing me as I rode his big dick. I unfastened his pants and had them down in no time. I wanted to get my mouth on that big cock. I almost gasped when I saw it for real in all its glory. It was perfect. It was not only long but it was wide. It was the kind of dick that size queens dream of—huge but not so big that you couldn't get it inside of you. I had fantasized about this kind of cock all my life and I was happy that I was finally going to have one. He stepped out of his pants and my lips were all over it. Even thought it was a little difficult to get my mouth completely around it, sucking it was a sheer pleasure. It was just such a beautiful specimen and the fact that he kept his pubic hair trimmed was also a turn-on. This was a guy who knew what women wanted.

I licked and sucked that heavy cock of his until I could feel him starting to rise off his feet. I backed off and he pushed me back onto his couch. He pulled my panties off and started to lick my pussy. He went immediately for the clit and I orgasmed a little almost instantaneously. It felt so good for his moist lips to be on me. As he licked more and more, I could feel myself building towards another one. I could feel that he was stroking his cock a little as he licked me and the thought of that big dick being stroked only made me that much hotter. He put in his finger and started sucking my clit the way I had sucked his cock and I exploded. I came so hard that I started moaning loudly. I couldn't help it. I could tell that he was pleased by the way he stepped up the pace. This was good because I was just getting started. I was still aching to get fucked.

I pushed his head away and pulled him into me. He was aware of how big he was because he entered me gently, but once he was in, I couldn't help but start fucking him hard. He filled me up completely. I wanted him take me and he did. I wanted him to fuck me like I needed to be fucked. I needed him to take me by force. It was a primal lust and he was more than willing to comply. He pumped me like he was getting all the sexual frustration and lust out that he had built up after his bad break up. I was fucking him the same way, fucking him so hard that it our skin was making a loud smack. It was amazing how much sexual energy a person can build up in the space of just a few months. Even masturbation had not dimmed mine and I could tell from how hard he was, his was at full force. With both of us fucking so hard, it wasn't long before I came again. However, he still wasn't done and I was only happy to get some more of his dick. I rolled over onto my stomach so he could fuck me doggie-style. This was my favorite position. It was one of the few things I could thank my ex-husband for getting me into. He had loved it and once he had talked me into doing it, I really liked the way it felt. He could penetrate me so much more deeply and could really hit my g-spot when he was fucking. Since Paul was so big, he was able to hit areas that had hitherto been untouched by man. My breasts swung as he pounded me and once again I was thankful for my big boobs. He was thrusting me so hard that it was almost taking my breath away. This was a man who knew how to fuck a woman. This was a man who knew how to fuck period. It was wonderful and I came again before I felt his body tense up and felt the warmth of him erupting into me.

I rolled over and smiled and I couldn't help but take a look at his heavy semi-hard cock, so big and so sexy, just lying there, all satisfied just like the both of us.

"So, how about that champagne," Paul asked, smiling. He looked quite smug at his performance. He had every right to be too.

"I know I'm certainly thirsty," I said, laughing.

We didn't even bother to put on out clothes back on because we knew that we would be having sex again. And we did several more times that day.

3

Of course, the next couple of weeks went by slowly. I couldn't wait to see Paul again. And more importantly, I couldn't wait to fuck him again. If seeing the couple in the alley had been a re-awakening of my sexuality, having sex with Paul that Sunday bordered on a life changing experience. I wondered how I had ever done without sex like that. I realized that if I wasn't careful, I could get addicted to fucking him. However, that was one addiction I could live with. I was horny all the time and I got wet just thinking about him and the things we had done. I couldn't help but give my vibrator a real workout. I knew that I was gushing like a schoolgirl but we had had a real connection. I know that he felt it, too. I knew it was too soon to really know where this was going, but it was fairly obvious that there was something substantial there. Even if this only happened to be a short term thing, I was sure that it was going to be a good one. Even if it was purely sexual. He phoned me several times through the week I guess to let me know that I did really mean something to him and that he wasn't a game player. I really appreciated that.

On Wednesday, Doreen and I went out to lunch at a deli near the office. Things had been so busy at the office that I had barely had time to talk to her. I knew that she was dying to know the details. All the details. She had a very dirty mind, but was so open with her own sex life that it wasn't really uncomfortable to talk to her about anything. But up until now, our conversations had usually been very one-sided. There had never been too much to talk about regarding my sex life with Eric, my ex-husband. So over reubens and bottled water, I told her the details.

"So what happened? How was your date?" Doreen asked, not even interested in the gigantic sandwich that was in front of her.

"It was great. We went to brunch."

"So did you fuck him?" she abruptly asked, smiling. "I bet he was good, wasn't he?"

I blushed a little and put my sandwich down. "Yes, we had sex." I thought for a minute. "And he was a lot better than good," I said. I wasn't really sure what else to say without actually coming out and telling her all the dirty details.

Doreen cackled. "I knew it! I knew that you were going to sleep with him from the minute you met him! I can tell these things. You two just had a real chemistry. I could see it. "

"I'll say," I said, getting a little more comfortable. "It was probably the best sexual experience of my life. He was good. He's also a great kisser. He really knows how to treat a woman. That's all I have to say."

"I bet he was big, too, wasn't he?" Doreen asked, her eyes growing larger.

I laughed and nodded. "You don't miss a thing, do you?"

She laughed again. "Tom's huge, so I can tell when a guy is packing and when he isn't. I couldn't help but check Paul out when he was sitting down. Whoo!" She mock fanned herself like she was getting overheated just thinking about it. "That man is packing some meat!"

"You know how some guys look better with clothes?" I said before I thought about it. I couldn't believe that I was being so open, but it was such a great experience for me that I just wanted to talk about it.

Doreen nodded.

"Well, Paul should go around nude all the time. He looks good in clothes and he looks even better without. I mean, he's like built. And that dick of his…" It was my turn to start fanning myself.

"Well, you're going to have to get me a picture then," Doreen said laughing. "He's European, you know. He probably won't mind. They're not ashamed of their bodies the way we are."

"Listen to you!" I said.

She laughed. "I'm sure that after Eric, he was a pleasant change."

"Doreen!"

"I'm just saying. I know that he wasn't really too heavy in the pants, if you know what I mean. I could tell."

"But he was good though," I said. I was telling the truth. While Eric wasn't the most endowed of men, he was a fairly good lover. Maybe a little too familiar that he became unexciting, but he usually could get the job done. I almost always orgasmed with him. However, looking back on it, sex with Eric had been almost like high school stuff compared to what I had experienced with Paul. It was like now I was really doing it, like I had been let in on what everyone else had been experiencing.

"Still. There ain't nothing like a big one."

She had a point.

We got back to eating our lunch. We had to be back at the office soon. But before we finished, Doreen stopped eating for a second and put her hand on my arm.

"I think he really likes you."

I smiled. "Well, I think I like him too."

She smiled again. "He texted Tom and told him. He thanked him for setting up the date."

I couldn't help but blush.

Doreen smiled broadly. "You deserve it, Elise. You deserve a good man for a change. You need something good to happen to you."

I smiled again. She was right.

4

As the time for him to get back into town neared, I was on pins and needles. I couldn't wait for him to get back. Especially after I had spoken to Doreen about him. I was so happy for her to tell me that he had said that he liked me. I was elated that I had found such a great guy. It was true that things were going really fast and that I was really falling for him, but I didn't care. He was almost too good to be true. He was so smart and good looking that anyone who knew him wouldn't have been surprised. He was the real deal.

Sex and him was all I could think about it. If I wasn't thinking about sex with him, I was reliving the various fantasies that had sustained me through my marriage. Fantasies that had been culled from romance novels and snippets of porn movies that I had accidentally caught my ex-husband watching.

This highly charged sexuality was so unlike me. My sex-drive had never been this strong. Sure, I was a normal human being, but everything had always been in its place. Sex in real life was nothing like sex in fantasy. It was much more boring and ordinary. However, after meeting Paul, it was like it had been let out of its cage and it was running wild. It was like my fantasy life had merged with reality and it really felt great. You have to realize what a big step this was for me to be so bold with my sexuality. As I said earlier, I married young and had only been with one person, Eric, my ex-husband. Now, this is not to say that I was a stick in the mud in the bedroom because I wasn't. Since we were so young, of course, our hormones were out of control and we did everything. I mean everything. And we did it everywhere. But of course most of this was before we actually got married. After we were married, however, things slowed down considerably. While I had given him a blowjob in a parked car in front of the mall one time just for kicks, it became almost a chore after we were married to even have regular sex in the sanctity of our own bedroom. It seemed that the burdens of being married, with all the responsibility of bills and work just wore us down and our sex life was the casualty. I was very hurt when he started screwing around on me, nevertheless I wasn't surprised.

But now, it was almost as if I had left the old me behind. Now I understood all those girls at the office who were going out every weekend and hooking up. It was just natural and before I couldn't understand how they could be so wild and incautious, now I got it.

This new boldness in me led me to do something that before I would never have even thought of. On the day that he was to arrive at the airport, I got made up and put on my sexiest high heels. Then, I got out my best black overcoat. It was a nice one that I rarely wore. It went down to about midthigh and fastened with only a belt. As I prepared to go out to meet him, I put on the coat. And nothing else.

Yes, I was going to meet him at the airport wearing nothing but the coat. I couldn't wait to do it. All my reserve was gone and I was so proud that I had come up with this little adventure. I had been preparing all week. I had gotten my hair cut and nails done. I had even gotten a Brazilian wax. I felt absolutely sexy and I knew that he was going to be happy to see me. As I walked out of my building to my car, I couldn't help but get wet. My big tits were barely concealed by the coat because only the belt kept it closed. Being so exhibitionistic was a real turn-on, I was finding. Also the fact that I was doing something so outside what I would usually do was also very hot. I got into my car and drove to the airport.

After I got to the airport, I walked in and found a good place to wait for him. I wasn't exactly sure which gate he was going to be arriving at so I found myself a central location so I would be sure to see him. As I walked around and waited, I could feel all a lot of eyes on me. I just knew that they could tell that I was naked under the coat. It was so exhilirating to know that just one layer of cloth was all that kept me covered. My nipples were erect from the excitement. Also, the fact that I could barely move without flashing either a bit of ass or tit was almost enough to make me run to the bathroom and masturbate. I was hot just anticipating the sex we were going to have that day. I knew that he was going to be surprised to see me. I knew that he was going to be happy. Then I saw him in the distance. When he saw me, he began to smile. I knew that I had been right.

"Elise, I'm so glad to see you. I was going to call you when I got to my apartment. But I guess now I don't have to." He was smiling from ear to ear. He was also looking me up and down. I could tell that he knew I was wearing something sexy but just how sexy was still an unknown to him. We kissed deeply for a few seconds and I could feel the electricity starting again.

I smiled and we walked out to my car. I couldn't wait to get him alone.

After we got into the car and started driving, I looked over at him and smiled, but didn't say anything.

"What is it?" he asked. "You're acting very mysterious."

"Aren't you going to say anything about my outfit?" I asked, knowing that this was going to perplex him.

"Oh, it's very nice, I'm sure. But I haven't seen it yet. You're wearing that coat."

I smiled again and opened the coat, showing my breasts and freshly waxed pussy. His breath quickened a little and he couldn't help but smile. I moistened my lips as I reached over and rubbed his dick. It hardened immediately. I simply had to unzip his pants and stroke him a little. I wanted to see it again in all its glory. Of course, it looked as great as I had remembered.

"You should wear this outfit more often," he said with his eyes slightly closed.

I hurried and drove to his apartment and we were all over each other as soon as we hit the elevator. We couldn't get at each other fast enough. Our mouths were on each other from the second we entered it. Just the small amount of privacy the elevator provided was enough. The door was barely closed before he was down on his knees and eating my pussy as I leaned back against the elevator wall, my coat falling to the floor. I came fast because I was so pent up from waiting on him all week. A couple of floors up, the door opened and an older couple was standing there waiting to get on. They couldn't help but see me there, completely nude and shuddering from orgasm while his head was still between my legs. They didn't get on and the door closed. I was sucking him by the time we were to his floor. I didn't want to stop so we held the elevator until I was finished.

"Oh, I've been wanting you so badly," he said breathlessly as I managed to deepthroat him a little. I didn't think it was possible but I did it. I just licked my lips and started sucking and before he even had a chance to think about it, he was in my throat. He gasped because he was so surprised. He was almost too big, but I was so filled with lust and horniness that I was willing to try. I could taste his precum almost immediately after I started doing it. I didn't want him to come just yet because I was ready for fucking. I had to have his dick in me. I needed his dick in me. I got up and stood against the elevator wall. Pants down around his ankles, he leaned in on me and entered me standing up, his enormous erection almost lifting me off the ground. Just like on the Sunday earlier, he fucked me hard, like he was getting out all the frustrations of the day. He knew just how I needed it. How I craved it. It was the stuff of my fantasies. I loved it. I loved this rough approach. I liked to be handled like that. To be taken control of. I liked to be hammered. My ex-husband, Eric, had never been able to fuck me like that for a sustained period of time like Paul could. He couldn't keep from coming. Paul and I fucked like that for a few minutes before a voice came over the intercom. It was the doorman asking if there was someone holding the elevator and if they were to please stop.

We laughed.

"Go ahead and finish, we'll fuck again after we have a drink," I said, breathlessly.

He grinned and pumped me hard a few more times before coming. It was a massive load and I could feel it warming the inside of my pussy as he released it into me. And after he had pulled out, I could feel it dripping down

24

the inside of my thigh. I was going to have to have more of this.

We left the elevator and walked over to his apartment. As he unlocked the door, he turned and looked at me. '

"I don't think I have anything to drink here."

I smiled. "Great, then we can start fucking again that much sooner."

5

The next few weeks flew by. We spent almost all our available time together. It was pure heaven for us. When we weren't going out to eat, visiting museums and going to concerts or just walking, we were having sex. And when we weren't having sex, we talked about ourselves. This is how we really got to know each other.

I learned that Paul was an only child and that his parents had died when he was a teenager. I also learned that when he hadn't been at boarding school, he had lived with an aunt somewhere near Amsterdam. I could tell that he didn't really like to talk about it, so I didn't press him. I also found out that he had inherited a lot of money from both his parents and grandparents. And that he was fairly close with a cousin in Belgium named Carolina. The great thing about him was that he didn't really even act like being rich was a big deal or anything. It was just something that was. It was in the background and wasn't something that people really needed to talk about or really think about either. In fact one time at a bar we overheard a guy talking about some big commission he had made on selling something. He was really hooting and hollering and bragging about it. Paul just sort of cringed. I could tell that he thought that the guy was really low-class.

But it was after sex that we really talked the most about the deeper subjects. These were the best times because we were truly connected then. This was when we really communicated. This was the time when we really talked. We would still be nude and in the afterglow and we would have the most wonderful conversations. One time after we had had a particularly hot session, we were lying in bed drinking coffee in our robes and he suddenly looked at me very curiously.

"What is it?" I asked.

"I was just wonderiing about something."

"What is it?"

"Why would any man ever get tired of you? Why would any man ever let you go?"

I blushed. He was always so sweet without even trying.

"Well, you don't know my ex-husband then."

"He must not be like anyone I know.

Paul was right. He probably didn't know anyone like my ex-husband. My ex-husband would never hang around a guy like Paul. He preferred guys like himself. Meatheads. Overgrown fratboys. Crude guys who were only concerned with making deals, watching sports, eating wings and drinking beer. A guy as good looking, intelligent and sophisticated as Paul would only intimidate him.

"You have to understand that I got married young," I explained, as if I was almost making an apology for Eric. "Neither of us had ever really had that many sexual experiences before we met. I was a virgin and he had had just one other girlfriend."

"So, you're saying that it was inevitable that he would become tired of you?"

"I guess, yes. But I was as tired of him as well."

"That's bullshit," he said. "If you love someone, you never get tired of them. You were probably not meant for each other."

"Maybe not, but what he did to me still hurt."

He looked at me, wanting me to go further, but not wanting to ask. I felt it was time that I let him know.

"I caught him cheating on me. I mean, I literally caught him in the act."

"Wow," he said.

"Yes," I continued. "I shouldn't have been surprised, and deep down I knew, but I didn't expect him to be so open about it. So disrespectful to me, you know what I mean?"

He nodded.

"He had also been criticizing me about not ever having sex. This was true, but it just never seemed to work out with us any more. I mean I still masturbated and fantasized a lot, but I just couldn't really bring myself to do it him any more. I mean, he wasn't the same guy as when we had met. When we were younger, he was a lot of fun, but as he got older he changed but not for the better. He became petty and selfish. I just didn't really like him anymore."

"What do you mean?"

I thought for a minute, trying to think of a good example. "It was mostly small stuff and probably a lot of it was in my head but one thing that he did towards the end of a marriage that particularly annoyed me was that in restaurants, it seemed that he always ordered stuff that he knew I wouldn't like."

"So he wouldn't have to share with you?" he asked.

"Exactly. It was like he made a point of ordering the weirdest thing on the menu just so that he knew that there was no way that I would want any of it. Stuff he knew I hated. I mean, I could have been just imagining it, but it happened so often that I don't think I was. He could never order just a hamburger, it had to be the buffalo wing, crabcake, oyster, sardine burger for him or something equally as weird."

"Maybe he liked the buffalo wing, crabcake, oyster sardine burger?" Paul asked, smiling.

I shook my head. "He was probably the least adventurous eater I've ever seen. If it wasn't cooked to death, swimming in grease or something you could heat in the microwave, he wasn't interested in eating it. I'm fairly sure that his whole 'gourmet phase' was just a manifestation of his resentfulness towards me."

"So how did you catch him? If you don't telling me," he asked.

I paused. I couldn't believe that this was still difficult for me to talk about. I took a deep breath and plunged in. "I walked in on him with her. I came home from work early because they sent us home because the electricity was cut off and I walked right in on him."

He chuckled a little bit and shook his head. "The electricity was cut off?"

His laugh lightened the mood and I couldn't help but laugh a little, too. "I know. It's like it was meant to happen. Somebody in accounting forgot to pay the bill. Anyway, I opened the door, heard all this grunting and groaning in the bedroom and there they were bare-assed naked and fucking. They were so into it, even after they saw me, they kept at it for a few seconds. The mattress was still squeaking. "

"Then what happened?" he said, not the least bit perturbed.

"They stopped, and here's the kicker. He asked me to join them."

"You're kidding?"

I shook my head. "No 'I'm sorry' or anything. Just an invitation."

"So did you join?" Paul asked, straightfaced.

I punched him playfully and laughed, "No!"

"He sounds like a real asshole," Paul said.

"Oh, he is alright." I paused for a second. "And you know what? Looking back, I should have joined in. I should have jumped right in there and took her over. I should have given him what he wanted and then when he was all happy and everything just dumped him. Like the next day."

"That would have been a pretty smooth move. Give him his fantasy, make him happy and then crush him."

"I know. But I was too emotional to think like that. I mean, of course, I've had those kind of fantasies about other women. Every woman does but I've never done actually anything like that before. But she was hot. She was 'my type' if you know what I mean. Every woman has one. If I was going to do it with a woman it would be someone who looks like her. Her name is Ginger if that says anythiing."

He nodded and sort of acted like he didn't know how to respond to this. I continued.

"Instead, I just left and cried. I called him the next day and told him it was over. At first, he said it was just a fling and that he wanted me back, but I didn't believe him. He was a horrible liar. I guess that's why he never even tried to hide it. The fact that he's still with that girl says just what a liar and sleaze he was."

"It does."

We sat there for a minute drinking coffee. I decided that since I had come clean about my relationship, he should too.

"So how about you?" I asked. "Why did you break up with your ex?"

He didn't say anything. I could tell that he still wasn't comfortable talking about it. However after a few seconds he answered, "She cheated on me. Or at least that's the way I looked at it at the time." He then sort of trailed off and stared at something off in the distance.

And that was all he said. I waited for him to say more, but he didn't. It seemed like it was still a little painful for him to talk about so I didn't push him. Even though I was intrigued, I figured he would tell me the details when he was ready. However, it had felt very good telling him my story. Sure, I had rehashed it a dozen times with Doreen, but telling him felt better. I felt almost like I had finally unloaded my burden. This was probably because the element of uncertainty was gone. Before I wondered if it had been me, if the reason why he had cheated was because I was so undesirable. Now I knew that it wasn't true. I was now appreciated by a much better man than my ex-husband. That was all the validation I needed.

I changed the subject and we got dressed.

6

It had now been three months. Three of the best months of my life. And they were much better than every good moment of my marriage combined.

I looked over at Paul across the table from me. He smiled. It was so romantic

We were at Il Duce, which for the moment was one of the hottest restaurants in the city. It really had the buzz going for it and was always packed. How Paul had managed to get us reservations on such short notice, I don't know. He had managed to even get us a private table in the reserved dining room.

We were going out not only to celebrate our three month anniversary (it sounded so ridiculous to the old married part of me, but also very sweet) but also to give him a big send off. He was going on an extensive business trip and was leaving for the next day. He was going to be conducting seminars and going to conventions all over Asia. I envied him. I had always wanted to go to that part of the world. He had offered to take me, but I wasn't able to get that much time off work on such short notice. He was going to be gone a month.

"I don't know how you did it, getting us in here, but I'm glad you did," I said raising my glass of wine.

He smiled. "Here's to knowing the chef."

"Here's to knowing you," I said back.

He chuckled and took a sip of wine.

So that was how he Paul had set this whole thing up so fast. He knew the chef. In addition to this, as the night went on, I began to figure out that the chef was also his conspirator in planning the evening because we never even had to order. The waiter would simply bring out the courses. It was like we were receiving a special VIP tasting menu. Nothing we were served was even on the regular menu and everything was absolutely delicious.

"Some of these dishes are still in the experimental stage," Paul explained. "The chef wanted to try them out on a more discriminating palate before he puts them on the regular menu."

I was tickled pink at this. This was not the sort of thing that ever happened to me before meeting Paul. I hated to always compare him to my ex-husband, but I couldn't help but be reminded of one time when Eric had accompanied me on a work sponsored employee appreciation dinner. It was held at this very fancy restaurant downtown and was first class all the way. Before we had left for the dinner, he had jokingly talked about how funny it would be if he started acting like a loudmouthed hick around all the people I worked with. He thought that it would be hilarious to see all those "uptight assholes" have to deal with somebody like that. I had just thought he was kidding and forgot about it and after we arrived, he acted quite normal, as if he really had just been joking. That is, until it was time for the main course, which just happened to be steak. After that, however, I knew that he was actually going to go through with his little scenario when he made a point of ordering his steak well-done and began to make a big deal out of making sure that the waiter clearly understood that he "didn't eat raw meat." I was so embarrassed that I could have fallen through the floor. All my coworkers were looking at him like he was some kind of idiot who had never been let out of his house before, but somehow they managed to keep their remarks to themselves. I was grateful that they didn't make an issue out of the way he was acting, but when he asked the waiter for ketchup to put on his well-done steak, I just hung my head in defeat. Even if I tried to tell them that he was just putting on and wasn't really like this, they would never have believed me. My coworkers now made no effort to hide their smirks and snickers. To make matters worse, Eric seemed to relish in this role that he created for himself. He was now "the Rube" and made a point of acting as uncouth and unsophisticated as possible. He then began to go on about how this "thing would be a lot better if he could just get some ranch dressing." He thought he was being funny, but he didn't understand or care that people were laughing at him and not with him. After that, it didn't matter how competent or sophisticated I was at work because I would henceforth be known as "the Rube's wife." What was worse was that he didn't care one bit what he had done to me. He thought it was funny. He then proceeded to get drunk and then throw up in the corner of the restaurant. He loved telling this story of his little ruse to his buddies at parties and at the sports bar. It really seemed that he had loved humilating me. I always suspected that he thought he was bringing me down a few pegs by acting so badly. I realized that was the day when I truly began to despise him.

I was so thankful that Paul wasn't like him. That he was sophisticated and would never do anything to embarrass me. This made me want him even more and I couldn't wait to get back to his apartment. This evening at the restaurant had only served to make me even hornier for him. Also the fact that I wasn't going to see him for another month was also reason enough to try to pack as much sex into the night as possible. Even though there was no way it would be enough to last until he came back.

After the last dish, the chef came out.

"I hope you liked it," he said in a thick French accent, smiling. I could tell that he was extraordinarily proud of the food and could tell from the way that the plates had come back clean that we had liked everything.

Paul introduced us and it turned out that he and Paul had actually worked together in a restaurant right after college. It was in Brussels. I found out that Paul had actually been a cook at one time.

"Why did you quit?" I asked.

"I hated cooking," he said. "I thought it would be good way to learn about the restaurant business. I found out that I didn't need that much first hand information for what I was trying to achieve. That's why I decided to go into finance, the money end of things. In fact, I financed George's first restaurant."

George, the chef, nodded. "He was an absolutely terrible cook. Disorganized and completely unmanageagle. And absolutely no passion for the kitchen."

"What can I say? It was an experimental phase for me," Paul laughed.

"But I must say that you were a very good financier," George added, laughing.

We talked for a little while before George offered to give us a tour of the kitchen.

I was intrigued so we went back. The place was clean, I'll say that. It was also loud. People were yelling and the pace was fast. Those line cooks were stirring and frying and moving with a military like precision. It seemed like controlled chaos. I was reminded a little of the time I had worked in fast food in high school where all the action and activity in the restaurant was swirling around the vortex of the almighty order and eventually everything always seemed to land in one place. Usually, it did anyway. This was much more advanced than that though. It was a very impressive operation and I could tell that George was very proud of every aspect of the place. He stopped by every station and introduced us as friends and told us a little bit about what was going on.

Eventually, we were led to the storage room but before George could tell us about all his fresh ingredients and where he got them from, his sous chef came in with a very freaked out look to his face. Apparently there was an emergency of some sort.

"Excuse me for a minute," George said hurriedly and smiled nervously. "I think one of the dishwashers is having a breakdown."

This left us alone in the storage room. It was all the opportunity we needed. We looked into each other's eyes and knew that we were both thinking the same thing. We were at each other in an instant. All that food and all the wine had only served to make us even more passionate than we already were for each other. As I kissed him, I could feel his dick against me. He was already erect. I knew I was ready too. George would be back soon we didn't have much time. I pulled my panties off and pulled his big cock out of his pants and he was in me in a second. There was no longer a need for him to be gentle. He didn't have to be. He knew I could take it. That I wanted to take it. He knew that I could handle him. Besides I was so wet that he slid right in. We hungrily kissed each others faces and necks as we fucked hard and fast standing up, right there in the storage room amid all the vegetables and ingredients. I turned around so he could fuck me doggie and I could help but come fast, breathing hard and writhing as that big dick of his rammed into me. I ground against him hard and it wasn't long before I could feel him blasting his come inside me.

"I love you," he said.

"I love you, too."

We had just managed to get our clothes straightened back up, when George came back in, breathing a sigh of relief.

"False alarm," he said and then stopped. He took one look at us and chuckled. "So I no longer have to just worry about the cooks and waitresses fucking in my storage room, I'm going to have to worry about the customers too!"

I blushed bright red, but Paul just laughed. "Maybe you should start renting it out by the hour since it's so conducive to lovemaking."

George laughed. "Maybe I should. It's definitely something to consider."

I still couldn't stop blushing. It was very exciting but also embarrassing to know that someone else knew that you've been fucking. I couldn't believe that I actually was turned on by the idea that he knew. It was just so naughty. I loved it.

However, George didn't even seem to care that we had been going at it like crazy just a few minutes earlier. "Let's go back out to the dining room," he said. "I have a great dessert ready for you to try." But then he added. "But I don't think it's going to top what you just had."

We all laughed. He was right.

7

Every thing was great for me, but then one day it happened. The thing that you know is possible, but don't think will ever really happen. Your ex moves on.

"I just wanted you to let you know that I'm getting married. To Ginger. I wanted you to be the first to know..."

I didn't listen to any more of it. I sat and stared at the answering machine. I couldn't believe it. I played it again.

The message hadn't changed.

It was from one of the last lingering sorespots in my life, my ex-husband, Eric. He was indeed getting married. I couldn't believe it.

I had to sit down. I was devastated. I had convinced myself that I was over him, that I no longer cared about him. It was true. In fact, I was over him long ago, but that wasn't what bothered me about the message. I guess what upset me the most was that it was proof that he was over me.

Yes, he was over me.

I went to the kitchen and poured myself a drink. I went back into my living room and sat down. I couldn't believe how much I was letting this bother me even though I was with a much better man, having much better sex and having a much better life. I couldn't believe that anyone would actually want to be with him. It was such a crushing blow. It only proved that he hadn't grieved at all over the demise of our relationship. It proved that he was truly happy to be free of me. I also began to have doubts. What if he wasn't really that bad? What if it had just been me? I knew that I was now on the road of self-torture.

 And why had he called me? Why did he want me to be the first to know? What purpose did that serve other than to upset me? What an asshole. He had stuck in the knife when he had cheated and now he was twisting it. He was doing it to torture me. Did he really hate me that much? It was so typical of him to do something so petty and inconsiderate. But the more I thought about it, I began to realize that it could have also been that he was asking for approval. He was always needy like that. He would do something bad and then try to get other people to help him justify it, to tell him that what he had done was okay. This always allowed him to bypass having to deal with whatever it was that he had done. It was so annoying. Regardless, he hurt me.

 I was a good thing that Paul was going to be gone to Asia for a month. I couldn't let him see me like this. Hopefully, a month would be enough time to get over the hurt I felt. Things were going so well with us and our relationship that I couldn't bring him down with my problems. And I was not going to allow Eric to get in between us.

 After the restaurant last night, we had gone back to Paul's place and had had sex all night long. I mean literally all night long. We had fucked in every way possible. I wanted him to get his fill of me. I wanted to give him enough head to last him through the weeks ahead. I wanted him to remember me fucking and sucking him, to give him fantasy material. I was also getting enough for myself. Enough of him kissing me, enough of his hands on my tits, feeling me up and fucking me. And licking me. I could still feel him on me. I even gave him a handjob on the way to the airport in the taxi, stroking him just to the point of orgasm.

The driver hadn't even turned around. He was too busy talking on his cellphone.

Paul had promised to call or email everyday or at least every other day as long as his schedule permitted. I knew he would too. Because he loved me. Unlike Eric, who could never find the time to call when he was away on business. He was always too busy at the strip club or drinking with "the boys." After the restaurant, Paul also told me that he had booked a trip for us to Amsterdam, the city where he had gone to live after his parents had died. We were going to go after he got back from his trip. I couldn't believe that he had gone ahead and done it. It really said something about what a great guy he was. I had mentioned earlier that I had always wanted to go and he had thought that he would surprise me with a trip.

"But you travel all the time," I said. "I would think that you would want to stay at home after such a long trip."

"It's nothing," he said. "Besides, it's next to Belgium. I'll show you where I lived as a child. It's almost like going home. You can meet my cousin, Carolina."

I couldn't wait for him to come back, but I could deal in the meanwhile. I would be okay until then. I was going to get over Eric's pending nuptials if it was the last thing I did. So what if he hadn't wanted me? So what if he was doing this just to get back at me? So what if he was only trying to get my approval? I could care less. What I had with Paul was real and what I had had with Eric was just puppy love.

Still the feelings of rejection were strong. You can't be married to someone and not feel hurt when they get remarried. I couldn't help but feel like I was a failure, like I was worthless. Like he had cast me away.

Like no man could possibly ever want me.

I went to the kitchen and poured myself another drink. I then broke down into tears. No matter how much I tried to concentrate on the positive aspects of my life now, I still couldn't get the idea out of my head that I wasn't good enough.

8

As the next week went by, I began to realize that I had been wrong about how it was a good thing that Paul wasn't going to be here for a month. I thought it would give me time to get over Eric getting remarried. However, it only made things worse. Not only was I trying to deal with the rejection caused by the announcement but I was also missing Paul. And the fact that he could only talk for a few minutes at a time didn't help. He was so busy. I didn't have the heart to put the whole story into an email. Why did he have to be gone for so long?

Of course, I had told him, but we didn't really have time to get into it. He seemed to understand, but he also wondered why I was so upset. He thought I should be happy that the guy would how truly be out of my hair. I tried to explain, but I think I was only giving him the impression that I was still hung up on Eric. I gave up and stopped talking about it with him. I wasn't going to let that fathead, Eric, ruin this relationship too.

At first I talked about it to everybody I knew, but I think everyone else was getting the same impression that Paul was. That I was jealous and still hung up on my ex-husband. So I stopped talking about it at all. No one else I knew had ever been in the situation I was. Everyone was either still on their first marriage or had never been married.

Since I couldn't talk about it, I thought about it all the time. This is the way it usually it works with something like that. It has to come out some way; if it doesn't, it just rolls around in your head constantly. It absolutely drove me crazy. I needed a diversion so I was extraordinarily relieved when Doreen invited me to a girls' night out a couple of weeks later. It was just her and a few people from work. We were going to go barhopping and just have a good time. It was going to be great. I also thought it might get the whole remarriage business off my mind. At least I hoped it would.

I couldn't wait to go. I put on a sexy little dress. I didn't have any unsexy dresses anymore. I didn't want Paul to think I was some sort of frump so I had gotten rid of all my dowdy clothes. All my "mom jeans" and loose work clothes had been thrown in the trash. Thanks to my new wardrobe, I looked not only current, but also sexy. That alone was testament to what a good relationship can do for you. I took a taxi over to the little Mexican bar where were going to meet. The girls were already there.

"Hey, Elise!" Doreen said as I walked over to her. "You look so cute!"

"You do too," I said. Doreen did look very cute too.

I said hello to the other girls and we sat down and started drinking. We ordered margaritas, of course, and began talking and eating chips and salsa. Pretty soon, I was feeling pretty good and all thoughts of what was going on in my life were quickly leaving my head. It wasn't long before I was only thinking about Paul and what I was going to do to him when he got back.

Let me stop here for a moment and say that alcohol makes me horny. Tequila especially so. It makes some people mean, but it causes me to be turned on. I like to joke that it was the only thing that kept my sex life alive for the last two years of my marriage. And let me just say, the margaritas were mixed quite strong, if you know what I mean. This is why I was beginning to think about sex with Paul so much.

Also the fact that I really missed him was probably playing into it.

So we were drinking and having a good time. Of course we talked about our favorite subject—how our men always let us down.

"My husband doesn't even know I'm around unless I'm putting dinner on the table," Marcie, who worked in word processing said.

"Mine thinks that just because he puts his beer cans in the trash that he really helps me out around the house," Darlene, who also worked in word processing added.

Doreen, of course, couldn't stand to be topped. "Well, Tom thinks that after we have sex...

"After you let him have sex with you, you mean," Darlene interrupted.

"Exactly," Doreen said laughing a little drunkenly. "He thinks that I should thank him for the orgasm!"

We all hooted at that.

After a while of drinking margaritas there we decided that we would switch bars. We walked to a little Irish place a few doors down.

We had a couple of drinks there, but Doreen and Darlene had to leave. I don't think the combination of the beer we were now drinking and the margaritas we had just had was sitting too well with them anyway. It was now just me and Marcie, who by this time was almost so drunk she couldn't talk. I, however, was still going strong even though I was pretty wasted. I wanted to drink! And I was still upright and I was horny as hell because of all the margaritas and from thinking about sex with Paul. Clearly, I wasn't thinking straight when two guys, who I later that night found out were in the Navy, came over to our table and offered to buy us drinks. Marcie could only nod and mumble at this point, but I said sure. In my inebriated state, I was sure that Paul wouldn't mind a guy buying me a drink. Besides it felt good to have the attention, especially after huge rejection I had felt from Eric. And the guys were also very hot. That's always an aid to conversation, especially when you're as drunk as I was.

It was pretty nice. Pretty soon, Marcie, passed out completely and was face down on the table. So it was just me and them. Their names were Johnny and Sonny and they were extremely good looking. They were muscular and tattooed and I couldn't help but feel very sexually attracted to them. Any woman would have. Due to the alcohol, I started to have some crazy thoughts. I thought about how it would be okay to fuck them and how Paul probably wouldn't mind. How he would understand the hurt I was feeling from Eric and how he wouldn't mind because he wasn't here with me. How he wouldn't mind me getting my sexual needs met by these two strangers in a bar. I know I sound awful, but in my alcohol saturated mind, I could hear him saying, "Go ahead and have fun, Elise. You're only young once."

I also started thinking that he was probably having sex with other people too. That he was probably with geishas and Asian hookers and women he met at the conferences. I thought about those women enjoying that big dick of his and I was over the edge. It made me jealous and horny at the same time. My breathing got deeper as I became more and more locked onto the idea of having sex with these two guys. The hottest thing about spontaneous anonymous sex is that at that moment everybody involved wants it so badly. They want it so much that they'll do it whatever the consequences. I was so horny that I kept crossing and uncrossing my legs, getting wetter by the second. I was doing anything in my mind to justify what I wanted. To get

42

fucked by these two sailors. Needless to say, we went out behind the bar into an alley about five minutes after that.

After we went out back, Johnny was kissing me hard while Sonny was behind me kissing my neck. I wanted it so badly so I reached around and started rubbing Sonny's cock through his jeans. He was hung. And hard. He knew what I wanted and unzipped his pants. This was purely sexual. Nothing but lust. No romance was involved. I pulled my dress up and he moved my panties aside and stuck it in. It was pure heaven. He started fucking me hard. Johnny pulled his pants down so his cock was out too. He was equally endowed as well, but thicker. I couldn't wait to get my lips on it so I bent over while Sonny pounded me and started sucking it. He smiled at me. I had gotten really good at this with Paul. Especially when a man had a really big, heavy dick. It was different from sucking a man with a small one. There was a lot more licking involved because it was just a bit more difficult to get it in my mouth. They were extremely horny, like they had been at sea for a while and hadn't been around a woman for a long time. They just couldn't get to me fast enough. I loved it. I loved being used like that. Like I was piece of meat for their pleasure. Occasionally people would walk by us in the alley, going to their cars and walking home. Some of them stopped and watched while others would hurry on not wanting to be voyeurs. I liked it when they stayed and watched. I remembered the woman in the alley I had seen on that first night with Paul and felt even more sexually alive. It only enhanced the experience for me. I played up my fucking for them. We went on like this and I orgasmed not long after that. It was a big one and I couldn't help but almost shudder from the spasms of pleasure I was feeling. If one big cock was good, two big cocks were better and I looked forward to more.

We switched out and it was a good thing because I was beginning to taste Johnny's precum. I came again, hard, and the sounds of ecstasy I made only made to make Johnny more turned on. It wasn't long before I could feel Johnny come inside me. Sonny, however still wanted to fuck. I turned around and he rode me like there was no tomorrow. Just like I liked to be ridden. I could feel my teeth chattering, he was fucking me so hard. He was powerfucking me and I surprised myself with yet another orgasm. It was another big one and came up on me before I expected it. This gave him about all he could take and he came all over my ass.

After we were finished, we straightened ourselves up and went back inside the bar and had another drink. We talked about the good time we had just had and had some laughs. We didn't bother exchanging numbers because we all knew that this was just a chance pick-up. Just a little fun. I felt really good and excited about it in my drunken state. I had never done anything like that and it felt good to be so sexual. And it was all due to Paul. Even though I had done everything in the world to justify having sex with the two sailors, I found that I did not want to think about him. But I did realize that he had done this to me even though he had done it inadvertantly. He had made me into such a horny woman. I pushed him out of my mind and just thought about the fucking I had gotten. I almost wanted to start masturbating at the thought of it, but decided that it was time to for me to go. The guys had to get back to wherever it was they were supposed to go. They joked that if they didn't get back they were going to get courtmartialed.

But before we all left, Marcie woke up and wondered where she was and what she had missed.

We laughed and told her that she hadn't missed anything.

I called her a cab and we all went our separate ways home.

I couldn't wait to get to sleep even though I knew the next morning was going to be hell.

9

My head was bursting the next morning. I was so hung over. My mouth was so dry that I felt like I needed to drink a gallon of water. However, when I remembered the fucking I had gotten by the two sailors, I couldn't help but be turned on. I could still smell them on me and this was more than enough to get me going. I reached to my nightstand and took out my vibrator and put it to my pussy. I was coming in a matter of seconds.

But then I remembered Paul.

My hangover vanished and suddenly I was dead sober. What had I done?

I had cheated on him is what I had done. I had done to him what had been done to me. And worse yet what had been done to him by his ex-girlfriend. I done something I had never even contemplated doing before and I had done it with random strangers. It was so unnecessary. I felt absolutely terrible.

I tried to rationalize. I hadn't felt any feelings for those two guys. It was just sex. It was just hormones. And besides I was drunk. And it had felt so good. So dirty.

I pushed that thought out of my head. I was angry with myself for even thinking it. How could I be like that? How could I be so low? I had done wrong. There was no excuse for my behavior. I didn't know what was wrong with me. But that was an easy question to answer. I had been rejected that's what was wrong. Eric had called saying he was getting remarried and it had destroyed me. I was so depressed that I should not have been left alone by myself. His calling me had brought me down and I had brought myself down even further by letting him get to me.

But I had Paul. Or at least I had before what had happened last night. Why had Eric gotten to me? Why had I allowed him to jeopardize my relationship? What about our trip to Amsterdam? I was so stupid. I wanted to cry.

I thought about Paul again. Maybe I could get away with not telling him. Maybe I could just bury it down and pretend it never happened. Could I do that? Could I keep it to myself? Nobody saw me fuck them. Nobody saw me with them. Marcie had been too drunk to know what was going on.

No, I realized, I couldn't lie to him. I would never be able to live with myself. If I didn't tell him, it would always be there between us, even if he didn't know exactly what it was that was on my mind. Besides I loved him too much. It would come out. But what would he do when he found out? Was it worth the risk? Shouldn't some things remain secret in a relationship? I was torn.

Still, all this was his fault, I thought a little sadly and smiled. Before him I had never been this sexual. I had never been so turned on. I had never known what sex could become. How it could change your life. I would have never even seen the possibilities that two guys like that could present. Sure, I might have fantasized about them later, but I would never have actually done anything with them. Before him, I would've run from them. I would have hidden in the ladies room until they left. And more importantly, I would never have accepted those drinks from them. I wouldn't have let myself get in to such a situation.

That was where I had gone wrong.

I went around and around with myself the rest of the day. I waffled between feelings of regret and horniness over the situation. I also waffled between wanting to tell him and keeping it to myself. I had no precedent as to what to do. I had never been in the situation before. The fact that I had been so angry with Eric for cheating on me only made me feel that much worse. I had chalked up his infidelities to the fact that he was a bad person. That he had been flawed as an individual. That he didn't really love me. But there was a difference between he and I. He was supposedly in love with the girl with whom he had had an affair. The two guys I had fucked had been random pickups. They could have been any two good looking guys. They were just in the right place at the right time. Also there had been two of them! I didn't even know them! I didn't even know their last names! His indescretions made him a cheater. What did mine make me?

A cheater. And a slut.

I sat down on my couch and sighed. I was now a slut. A nympho. It made sense. All these factors had gone into it, but the main thing was that Paul had awakened something in me. He had done it with his big cock and the fact that he knew how to fuck. He knew how I liked it and he was man enough to do it. Bluntly speaking that it.

I had no one to blame but myself. I knew that if Paul and I broke up over this, I would probably do stuff like this all the time. The door had been opened. The switch had been flipped. I had lived through a sexless marriage before and there was no way I was going back to it. Even though I felt horrible about it, and even though I had hurt Paul, I wanted to do it again. I wanted to have sex again with random guys. I wanted to have sex in public again. But I also wanted to keep having sex with Paul. In other words, I just wanted to be fucked. It was like it had finally dawned on me that I was addicted to sex, to cock. It was like I had dabbled with it before Paul, but once I got a taste of the good stuff, I was hooked. But this was an addiction that I didn't want to kick.

I loved Paul. I really did. I wanted to protect him from what I had done, but I knew it wasn't possible. I had to tell him. I had to explain. This was just too big of a thing to keep locked away in my mind. He had to know what I had done. I knew that he would probably drop me and I would be devastated. He had to know. All I would be able to offer him other than my apology was the promise that I wouldn't do it again. I would also assure him that that I would rein in the slut. As long as he was fucking me I knew that I could. He was just that good. He would be enough to satisty my lust. I would tell him everything. Especially how much I loved him.

That's all I could do. That, and hope for the best. But I knew that most likely the relationship was over. And it was all my fault. I started crying. However, it was all I could do to fight the temptation to go back to the bar to see if those guys were there again.

10

It was difficult but I did it. Paul did nothing but sat there stonefaced, still trying to process what I had just told him. I had told him everything and now he was just sitting there without saying anything.

Paul had gotten back into town the previous night and we had gone out to dinner. I didn't want to immediately overwhelm him with the story of my indiscretion, so I waited for the right time. It was hard to hold back especially when he started talking about our trip. I just wanted to get it over with, but I knew I had to restrain myself.

I waited until after dinner at my place the following night. When we were alone. I wanted him to have space so that he could scream, freak out, call me a slut or anything else he wanted to do. I felt so badly before I did it. He was not expecting it at all. He was smiling and telling a story about something humorous that happened at a hotel in Tokyo when I told him. A guy had thought he worked there and had demanded that he take his drink order. He had threatened to turn Paul in to the manager of the hotel if he didn't comply. Later on, the fellow was shocked to find out that Paul was the main speaker at the conference the guy's company was sponsoring that evening. It was actually a funny story, but I had no choice but to ruin it. It was time and I just blurted my confession out. I told him about Eric calling, about how horny the sex with him had made me, about me getting drunk on tequila, and how I ended up fucking those two guys. I told him about how horny I had been without him. I also told him about how much I loved him.

He had sat there, expressionless, and not saying a word.

"I'm so sorry, Paul. I was depressed. I was drunk. I wasn't thinking properly," I pleaded. "I won't do it again!"

He continued to sit there.

I went on about how he was the only man I wanted. About how I needed only him and he had awakened me sexually. I was careful not to say anything that would make him think I was blaming him for what had happened, because it really was all my fault. I didn't want him to think I was trying to avoid the responsibility of what I had done. I said it more as a tribute to him so he would know just how much I was indebted to him. I told him about how much I wanted to be fucked by him now. I told him just how much

I craved his cock and how he had opened my eyes to how great sex could be.

"Those guys meant nothing. They were just warm bodies. They were nothing to me. It's you I care about."

He stood up then and looked at me. "I have to go for a walk. I'll be back."

I started crying. "Please don't leave me! I couldn't help it!"

He didn't try to console me. "I'll be back."

I tried to grab him, to keep him from going, but he shrugged me off. I started screaming at him. "Don't leave me!"

He just stared at me, expressionlessly. Then he left.

I fell to the floor and sobbed.

. . . .

Three hours later, he came back. I was still in the same position on the floor as I had been when he had left. I was still crying. I was sure that he was gone for good and I was shocked when I heard him opening the door. At first I didn't believe it. I thought maybe I was dreaming. That maybe I had lost my mind. But when he walked into the room, I knew I wasn't.

"C'mon, Elise," he said, stooping down to me. "Get up and stop crying."

"But I thought you were leaving me!" I said.

He helped me up. "I said I would be back. Didn't you believe me?"

"No," I said. "Why would you come back? I cheated on you."

He maneuvered me over to the couch. "I understand, Elise. I understand."

As we sat down there together, he put his arm around me.

"I'm sorry," I said. "You don't understand how sorry I am."

"I know you are," he said. "I know that you didn't mean to hurt me. It was just something that happened. I know that you're not a cheater. That's what I've been thinking about. About this situation."

"What do you mean?" I asked. "Whatever I have to do to make it right, I'll do."

He shook his head as if he was telling me to stop apologizing. "I did a lot of thinking while I was walking around.

I listened.

"You know that I told you how my girlfriend had cheated on me and that was why we broke up?"

"Yes," I said, feeling even worse. It was all he had ever said about his breakup. He had never really given any more details than this. I knew how much he had been hurt and started crying again and apologizing.

"There's no need to cry," he reassured me. "The reason why I bring this up is because I've always thought that maybe I didn't handle it right. I was too embarrassed to talk about it because I have always felt very badly about how I acted and what I did. I've always wondered what if I had looked at it differently. What if I hadn't been so closeminded about the whole thing? What if I had been more accepting?"

I was taken aback. "You mean, you think you should have let her cheat on you?"

"No," he said, emphatically. "That's not what I'm talking about. Cheating is wrong, but what if I was just looking at it wrong. Maybe she wasn't really cheating. I mean, what if I had looked at her for what she was, a girl who loved sex."

I still didn't understand.

51

"She was a lot like you. She loved sex. Especially after we started going out, she said. I think I brought it out in her like I have you. She wanted to have sex all the time. But I think that after a while she couldn't control it. However, my problem was I couldn't handle it. I couldn't handle what I had made her. I was jealous and I didn't understand it. I was petty and couldn't see the big picture. I looked at the situation the way a normal person would, however, it was not a normal situation. Do you understand?"

"I think so," I said, not really knowing where this was going.

"Anyway, she really loved me and like you she apologized profusely, but I told her that I couldn't take the cheating and the lying that she was doing. I wasn't a man to be cuckolded."

"Are you saying that now you are?"

He looked at me very sternly. "No, I am not a man to be cuckolded. However, I know that I love you and I don't want to let you slip away from me over something so silly as you having sex with those two guys. Especially when I know that you really enjoyed it."

"But…!" I protested.

"Elise, I know that you liked it. There's no need for you to deny it. If you loved them, it would be different for me. I would be more upset. But I know you didn't. I know it was just about the sex. I know that you loved fucking them. It felt good for you. You love sex. You're almost a nympho now. And I know that I've brought it out in you."

I tried to protest again, but then conceded. I knew he was onto something. "It's true. Having sex with you really woke me up," I said, feebly trying to make a little joke. "You're just so damned good. Sex with you is the kind of thing women fantasize about. You made me crave sex."

"No," he said. "This need in you was already there. I just brought it out. If you had been fucked properly before, you would have been this way a long time ago."

He was right. Good sex had made me into one dirty girl.

"Anyway, to be with a girl like you one either has to expect to be cheated on or to leave. I want to do neither. There has to be another option. That's what I was thinking about as I walked."

"What do you mean?"

"I will not be cheated on and I will not leave you. However, I know that while you will always have good intentions you will have sex with other men. You will not be able to help yourself. You will go through periods of abstaining and then I will go away on business you will get so horny that you will succumb."

"Are you saying that I cannot control myself?" I said a little irritatedly.

"Yes," he said matter of factly. "As I told you, I have been through this before."

I tried to protest and say once again that I wouldn't do it again and that I could control myself.

"No, no. That's where you're wrong, Elise. Sex doesn't work like that. It doesn't matter how badly you don't want to do it or how bad the situation is for you, once you get turned on, all that's out the window. Each experience is a new one. You will not tire of it. You will want more and you will do it again. Even more so. It's just the way humans are. Besides, do you really want to deny yourself something you love?"

I didn't know what to say.

"So, I have been walking and trying to rationalize a solution, about how can we resolve this issue. I love you too much to let you go. I know how sexual you are now and how even if you were able to control yourself, I know how unsatisfied you would ultimately be."

"But you're all I need, Paul. You're more than enough for any woman."

"For now. But you'll get bored with me. Sure, the sex will be hot, but you will want to wander."

"So what can we do?" I asked.

He paused and looked me squarely in the eye. "I want you to submit to me."

"Submit? I asked. "Like with whips and chains, that kind of thing?"

He rolled his eyes. "No, I am not a sadist. And I'm sure that you're not a masochist. What I want you to do is turn yourself over sexually to me. Completely. I will direct your sexual encounters. You will let me control you sexually."

I still didn't understand.

"For all matters sexual, you will defer to me. I will tell you who you are to have sex with and how you will have sex with them. I will provide you opportunities to fulfill your needs and desires. I will help you live out your fantasies. If you have someone of your own in mind, you will ask my permission if you want to have sex with them."

My head was spinning from this. "I'm not sure if I understand. This is just a little weird."

"I know it is. But it is the only way our relationship will work long term. I will not allow you to cheat on me behind my back."

"But isn't this kind of the same thing? Except you're telling me to do it?"

He stared me right in the eyes again. "No, it is not. Cheating is dishonest. This isn't. If I'm directing you to do it, you are just doing what I say. You are not doing anything I don't know about and approve of. All you have to do is trust that I will not make you do anything that will hurt you or

54

that you will regret. Remember, I know you sexually. I know what you want."

After hearing it put this way, the idea began to intrigue me a little. Still, it was against everything I had ever been taught. Such behavior went against my upbringing. This was a hard thing to overcome.

"But don't you think this is just a little…trashy?" I asked. "I've never done anything like that before. I mean, who's to say I'll even do it again?"

Paul shook his head. "What does that mean? Trashy? You cannot go through life caring about what other people think. And you know that you'll do it again. And if you don't, you will want to so badly that it will make you miserable."

I didn't say anything but I agreed.

"Do you want a happy relationship, Elise?" he asked. "If you're not happy sexually, you'll not be happy in this relationship. I'm only trying to solve that problem."

"Can I back out if I don't like it?" I asked.

"Of course, and we can try it the normal way. But I can already tell you how it's going to end."

I looked at Paul and realized how much I wanted to be with him and how much I wanted him to be happy. And I wanted to be happy too. I really had something special with him and I was not going to let him go because of I had done something stupid and fucked those two guys. A relationship like this didn't come along everyday. Also, deep down, I knew he was right about me. I knew it from the minute he had said it. I knew it before he had said it. I knew it after I had fucked those two bozos.

"Okay, I'm in."

He smiled. "Great, then let's start talking about Amsterdam."

"Okay, I said, but let's get started on your plan. What do you want me to do first?"

He looked at me curiously for a second and then smiled. "Take off your panties. From now on, you will wear no panties. A girl as horny as you should never wear panties."

I immediately started feeling horny. I complied and from the wetness I felt, I knew that maybe he was onto something.

11

In the week that followed before we were to go to Amsterdam, I began to get more of an idea of what Paul was expecting me to do. And I could tell I would like it.

Okay, I'll admit in the beginning, when he first told me about it, I had my trepidations. I thought that he might be some sort of pervert or something, that he was just a bit twisted in his thinking. But I was the one who had fucked two random guys and he had done nothing, so what right did I have to judge him? Besides, I was willing to do whatever it took to make things right with him again.

So I decided to trust him. Also, I knew there was a lot of truth to what he was saying and a breakup was probably inevitable anyway, so why not give this one thing a shot? I loved him so much I didn't want to go down without fighting for what I wanted. And you know something? I found my first instincts had been right. Paul was sort of a pervert. But it was in a fun way and I loved it. I found that I liked his form of perversion. It was always centered around me and my sexuality. Through this, I also found out that I was a pervert too. And it was okay. It was okay for both of us to be this way.

Now we didn't go full bore into anything serious at first. I mean, Paul didn't start me gangbanging right off the bat. He was started me out easy, like he was building me up to bigger things. For example, after we fucked at his apartment on the day I broke the news about my infidelity, we went out. Of course, since he insisted that I stop wearing panties, I went without underwear. He also told me not to wear a bra either. I protested about the bra because my breasts were so full that they seemed to develop a mind of their own if I didn't keep them constrained. He objected, saying that this was the point. He wanted them to be on display. He wanted me to show them off the way they deserved to be seen. I complied with this request and, as I prepared to get dressed, I couldn't help but feel elated at the freedom I was feeling by turning over these decisions to him. It was something I would have been too uptight to do on my own. Of course, it was a thrill for me as it would be most women. To push things even further, he also insisted that I wear my shortest skirt and my lowest cut top. He said that he wanted me to show off "my assets."

Instinctively, I protested. I mean after all, I wasn't wearing any underwear. Wasn't that enough? Did I have to go this far with the revealing clothing? "But I'll really look like I'm on display."

He just stared at me with a knowing look and then I remembered.

"Oh," I said. "I guess I will have to do it since you're telling me to, right?"

"Elise, it's okay for you to do this now. I'm saying it's okay so it's okay. You can be yourself. Stop hiding your beauty. You know that you want to do this."

He was right. I did. The excitement I had gotten just from thinking about getting dressed in this way was enough to let me know that. I just never would have had the courage to do it without him telling me.

So I got dressed. Or rather "undressed" as we joked about it later. This was because I was now wearing less clothes than I had been previously and we went out.

Because we were planning on drinking, we took a taxi to a bar a couple of streets over. I felt so alive with my breasts out and bouncing and my pussy and ass just barely concealed. I found that I wanted people to look at me. I wanted heads to turn and mouths to drop which is exactly what happened when we entered the bar. All eyes were on me until I sat down. I could tell that every man in there wanted to fuck me. Every woman was either jealous or wanted to fuck me too. I felt great. We walked over to a table in the corner and once we got settled, Paul took a look around the room. He noticed that one guy in particular was staring at me. He was sitting on the other side of the room.

"Elise, open your legs so he can see your pussy."

I looked at him like he was crazy. It was one thing to be suggestive as I was doing by the way I was dressed, but it was another thing just to flash sombody. I didn't know if I was ready to go that far. But then I remembered what I promised Paul. If I was going to give this a shot, I needed to go through with it. I needed to submit to Paul's suggestion.

I turned and forced myself to look at the guy and smiled. He blushed. Then, breathing hard, I pulled my skirt up a little seductively and showed him everything. I was surprised at how easy it was once I did it. Now I wanted him to look at me. I wanted him to get an erection. I leaned over so he could get a good look at my cleavage as well.

At first he turned away embarrassed. Instinctively, I wanted to turn away too, but Paul stopped me. "He'll turn back around. He's a man. He can't help himself. You've done nothing to be ashamed of. He wants to see this."

Of course, he was right. The man turned back around, but this time he maintained eye contact. He just sat there and stared at me and my pussy. I could see him fidgeting in his pants and licking his lips. He was getting turned on. I don't know why, but this automatically made me wet. It was almost as if the fact that he was turned on made me turned on. It was a wonderful feeling. Next, he did something that I hadn't anticipated. He actually started rubbing himself through his pants. Now, I turned red. This was just getting creepy. Sure, this was the logical place for this kind of scenario to go, but it was difficult to fight years of conditioning. After all, I had been taught that when a man starts masturbating in front of you in a public place, you're supposed to run or call the police. You're not supposed to like it. Regardless of what Paul had said, I couldn't help but start to feel a little ashamed.

Paul sensed what was going on so he took control.

"Now, Elise, start rubbing your pussy. Let him know just how wet you are."

"Paul! Here! In front of everybody! I'll get arrested. This is just too much for me!"

"Do it. No one will care. A woman can get by with all sorts of things in public. Especially if she's as good looking as you. Do it and you'll feel good. You'll get over these feelings of embarrassment you're having right now."

"But what if someone I know sees me?" I hissed.

"No one here knows you. Now rub it. It's the only way for you to move forward."

Paul was so authoritative and convincing that I began to do it even though I was no longer feeling it. I began to masturbate right there in the bar. Of course, I was under the table so unless one was really looking they couldn't see anything. I'll admit that I wasn't too turned on at first, but when I saw the guy speed up his pace on his masturbation across the room, I began to warm up again. Paul had been right about the situation. I began to get more and more turned on and I no longer felt ashamed. The guy was really rubbing, too. Our eyes were locked as we masturbated across the room. I could tell that he was going to come soon all because of my pussy and my tits. This thought really struck a chord with me and I could feel my pulse quicken. I could feel the orgasm coming and it was on me before I knew it. It was hard for me to stifle my moans of ecstasy as I came. I felt great.

After I was done, I started to pull my skirt back down.

"No, leave it up," Paul said. "Don't be ashamed. You have a beautiful pussy. Show it off."

I looked over at the guy to see what he was doing now. He was no longer there. He had left, apparently too embarrassed to stay. Then I knew what Paul was talking about. There was no need to be self-conscious about sex. I was feeling really good about what I had done so why hide myself now? I was also pleased with myself that I had gone through with it. I had thought that my orgasm would bring on feelings of shame, but I had been wrong. I wanted to do again.

I was really beginning to get hot and bothered and I could tell Paul was too from the looks of the bulge in his pants. The outline of his penis was quite visible as it began to grow down the inside of his thigh.

So we went home and fucked. We were barely able to make it into his apartment before we were all over each other. Kissing and then fucking and sucking. He pounded me good and I came the first time just from the initial penetration. We did that until we were exhausted. I guess because of the sheer naughtiness of what I had done that night, I really wanted him to come on my breasts. So after he had fucked me for a while and was ready to come, I put his dick between my breasts so he could tit fuck me. I almost orgasmed again from the feel of his stiff hard cock thrusting between my boobs. I had to start rubbing myself and when he blasted all over them, I came again. He smiled from ear to ear. I was ready for more and I couldn't wait to go out again.

. . . .

Paul had to do a lot of work the following week so I didn't get to see him as often as I would have liked. However, in the meanwhile, he gave me what we began to call "assignments." These were what we called the dirty tasks which he told me to do. That week, since we couldn't go out together, I was supposed to do something dirty each day on my own. He would call me every day to remind me. One thing he ordered me to do was to masturbate every day at eleven and one o'clock regardless of what I was doing or where I was. If I was in a meeting. If I was at lunch. If I was getting my hair cut or nails done. Regardless. I was supposed to stop everything and get myself off. At first this was a little tough because it was hard to find a private place where I could whip out my vibrator, but I quickly solved this problem. I went to a sex shop and bought a personal strap-on butterfly vibrator that I could wear under my clothes. All I had to do was put it on and when the clock struck eleven, I just had to hit a switch. A few seconds later and I was there. I'm sure that many of my co-workers thought I was going through menopause or something because of how flushed I would get. At first I had thought this little assignment was a bit silly, but I soon began to watch the clock because I couldn't wait for these times to roll around.

He also ordered me to flash men and women in public places. After my experience at the bar, I really began love this and it almost became second nature. I also started wearing really low cut tops under my business suits. This way, I could whip off my coat and flash the tops of my nipples along with my pussy whenever I felt like it. I have to say that while some people were a little shocked when I would show them what I had, most were more than a little intrigued. Even the women. I was finding that the world was much more perverted and naughty than I had ever realized.

I just did stuff like this. I think Paul didn't want to me to do anything too major because he didn't want to miss out on any of the big stuff. But soon enough, we were able to be together again. Friday arrived and we went to an open air concert at the park. We were leaving the next evening for Amsterdam so we thought that this would be a good way to celebrate our upcoming trip. Also, since we had met at a concert at the park, it was also a little nostalgic for us.

We arrived at the park and immediately went to the beer stand. As most people know, alcohol is a very important part of outdoor concerts, because it makes the mosquitoes and heat so much more bearable. Also, it makes bland music that much more interesting. Of course I was dressed as slutty as the law would allow. Now Paul didn't exactly want me to dress like a hooker. This wasn't his thing. Aside from the low cut tops, Paul wanted me to dress in normal short skirts and regular clothes. He said that if I looked like a prostitute it made me look like I was selling something. He said he wanted me to look like I was giving it away.

"You look like a woman who wants to share her body," he said, feeling my tit as he sipped a cup of imported beer. "You look a woman who doesn't have to use sex for anything but pleasure."

I was flattered.

He continued. "The trouble with a prostitute is that because she wants you to pay her for sex, it makes it seem as though she doesn't really want to do it. If you give it away, it shows that you really enjoy it."

Very philosophical, I thought. And dead on. I definitely enjoyed sex.

Anyway, as the night progressed, the musicians warmed up and really got going. Pretty soon a rather large crowd had amassed around us. As the music started, I noticed that Paul was standing behind me and rubbing up against me to the beat of the music. I got wet. I could feel his hard cock grinding against me. I wanted it in me. I reached down and rubbed it. He responded by grinding even harder. Then I tried to unzip him. He stopped me, but kept grinding.

"No, Elise, this is Frottage. You don't pull it out. We can't have sex here. We would be mobbed."

"Frottage?" I asked rubbing my ass up against that big dick of his.

"Frottage. It means 'rubbing.' We do it in Europe. It's like dry humping but we do it in public," he said as he buried his head in my hair and kissed my neck. "You can do it right in front of most people and they don't know what's going on. They think you're just standing next to someone or dancing."

"Oh," I said, breathlessly and kept grinding against his dick in time to the music. I pulled my skirt up so that Paul could grind against my naked ass. My hand went to my pussy and I started rubbing it. I was juicing pretty heavily and I couldn't resist bringing my hand up to my mouth so I could taste myself. I came pretty quickly and I was ready for another one. I started grinding again and rubbing my clit with my other hand. I happened to glance over and noticed that Paul was no longer behind me. He was now standing beside me. He smiled at me and raised his beer.

I quickly looked around. Another guy was rubbing up against my ass and had a very intense look on his face. He smiled at me. "Frottage," he said softly with a French accent. He was obviously a foreigner. And very good looking. I ground back against him, getting hotter from the feeling of the stranger's humping on my unclothed ass. He quickened his pace and it was just a couple of seconds before I could feel him orgasm on me.

I couldn't help but laugh. "Frottage indeed," I said and rubbed myself to even bigger climax. It was such a naughty thing to be doing in full view of anyone who cared to see that I couldn't help but get even more turned on by it. I couldn't wait for what Paul had in store for me next.

12

I was excited about going to Europe again. Other than a short business trip to London and a high school chorus trip to Italy, I had not had much of an opportunity to truly experience it. I had always been constricted by either chaperones or time. Also, I knew that I was going to hit the ground fucking when we arrived in Amsterdam. And I was right. Within just a few hours I was face deep in an Australian backpacker's pussy and was loving every minute of it. It was my first time with a girl and I knew that it wouldn't be my last. Also the fact that her boyfriend was fucking me also didn't hurt things either.

We had picked them up, or rather they had picked us up, at a hash bar in the Red Light District. Before we had gone out Paul had told me to get ready to get fucked because it was going to happen tonight.

"Why are you so sure?" I asked.

He laughed. "It's Amsterdam. It's a party city. Everybody here wants to get laid or high or both." He paused for a second. "Except the locals," he added.

According to him, even though Amsterdam was known as one of the marijuana smoking capitals of Europe, most of the people he knew there had never touched the stuff. He said that most of them were actually very normal sorts of people. "Besides Amsterdam is not like the rest of Holland," he said. "It might as well be another country."

This actually led to a funny incident in a bar that happened just prior to us getting picked up by the Australians. A group of unibrowed, doughy American frat boys were talking and one of them said that everybody there was on drugs. He also said that basically the whole country was like the Red Light District. Completely ridiculous stuff. Paul overheard this and, not wanting the country to be misaligned, told them that the rest of the Netherlands was actually fairly conservative and not anything like Amsterdam.

The frat boy looked at him like he was crazy. He actually began to lecture Paul in a very consdescending way. "That's the problem with Americans. They don't travel and they know nothing about the world. I've been to Amsterdam twice so I think I know a little more about it than you do."

Paul shook his head and chuckled. I guess his accent was so good that the guy had mistaken him for another American. I couldn't help but crack up laughing. I'm sure that the frat boys assumed we were on drugs too, just like everybody else. Oddly enough, we later saw that guy running around the Damstraat feverishly looking for his passport. Apparently, someone had stolen it from him while he had been at that bar lecturing Paul.

We had flown all night and got there early in the next morning. Because Paul had flown this trip many times before he said that we needed to sleep as much as possible. He said that these night flights seemed to be engineered to completely screw up your body so the best way to avoid this was to sleep. He even brought along some over-the-counter sleep medication which we took before we even got on the plane.

"But what about the mile-high club? How can I join if we're asleep?" I asked.

"We'll do it on the way back," he said. "I want you to be feeling good when we get there."

Apparently he knew what he was talking about because, thanks to the medication, I fell asleep right after we boarded and didn't wake up until they were serving breakfast. In fact, Paul and I seemed to be the only bright eyed and bushytailed ones as we landed at Schipol.

We took a train to the city and went to our hotel which was fairly close to Central Station. Paul said that in order to really have a good time here, we needed to be able to walk everywhere. We didn't want to have to fool around with figuring out the trolleys or catching taxis once we started drinking.

Of course, we fucked as soon we got to the room. I couldn't help myself. I was so horny and the thought of being in a new city was too much. Especially a city like Amsterdam with its emphasis on partying and sex. Paul was feeling the same way too because he basically tore my clothes off and was fucking me doggie style before I knew what was going on. He rammed me so hard he took my breath away. We didn't even bother with the foreplay because we were that horny. I came pretty soon because of his big cock. He really filled me up and hit my g-spot easily. I wanted to suck him off, so I got down on my knees and gave him head. I licked and sucked and deepthroated until I could feel him start to tense up. When his testicles clenched

I got ready for the load. I then licked until I could feel him shooting his hot semen in my mouth.

With that out of the way, I was ready to go sightseeing.

We left the hotel and did the touristy thing that first day, waiting for night to come. I was horny with anticipation because I knew that I was going to have some sort of sexual encounter. I wasn't sure what, but Paul had said as much earlier. The mystery of it was a huge turn-on. There was no telling where the sex would take me in this strange, new country. Still, I enjoyed the sights. We went to Anne Frank's house and toured the Heinekin facility. I got a bit drunk there because we went before we had had a chance to eat. We also looked at some windmills and ate Thai food, but mostly we walked and talked. As we toured the Rembrandt House Museum, I began to notice that there was something odd with Paul going on. It was the fact that even though we were in Holland, Paul always spoke English everywhere.

"Why don't you speak Dutch here? I would think that since it's your first language, you would like to speak it," I asked.

"Why? Everybody in Amsterdam speaks English."

It didn't really make sense to me, but I went along with it. It only made things easier for me to understand.

We walked around some old neighborhoods and then we went back to the room and rested. When we awoke a couple of hours later, it was night. It was time to party.

So, we got dressed. Even though it was summer, it was still a little chilly there so I had to wear a coat. I still managed to wear a very short skirt and a low-cut top underneath along with some heels. I was not quite on display as I would have liked, but I still felt very sexy.

We left the hotel and walked down the Damstraat and then went to the Red Light District. At the edge of it, we stopped and had a beer in a bar where a group of people were singing Dutch folk songs. Paul even joined in on a few much to the surprise of the customers there. They had thought he was an American as well. We then left and walked around and went into a few more bars. One of these was where we encountered the lecturing fratboy. As we made our way more deeply into the Red Light District, it was like culture shock for me. I couldn't help but crack up when I saw the open air street urinals on the corner. Paul, of course, didn't see anything odd about them at all.

We walked around, looking at the girls in the windows and browsing through the sex shops. I felt at home here. I felt alive. The sex was palpable and seemed completely normal here. I looked around at all the tourists and people walking around and wondered if they felt the same way I did. If they were as turned on and at home? I doubted it. Meanwhile I was getting hornier and more anxious. Was he going to make me go into one of these brothels? Was he going to make me strip off in public? What was he going to do? I almost wanted to start rubbing my clit I was so horny with anticipation.

Then we walked into this hash bar, the Bullfrog, and I knew it was going to happen here at this place. I could feel it. I didn't know exactly how, but I knew this was it.

The place was filled with young backpackers. There were groups and couples sitting around smoking weed. Paul said he was going to order some which surprised me a little since I had never seen him smoke even a cigarette.

"I wonder what is the smallest amount I could buy?" he said aloud before we sat down.

"We'll share with you," the Australian couple said from the booth next to us. "If you care to join us. There's no way we're going to be able to smoke all this."

Paul looked at me and smiled. I knew that this was going to be it. We were going to have sex with them.

"Sure," Paul said and we sat down with them.

They were stoned and after I finished smoking just a little, I was fairly stoned too. Paul didn't seem too affected though. It was pretty obvious what the Australians had on their minds after just a few minutes in. They were picking us up. I didn't mind because they were both very attractive. They were blonde, both in their mid-twenties and were very athletic looking and tanned, like they spent a lot of time at the beach. The guy, Nathan, was an engineer and the girl, Lucy, was a school teacher. They lived together in Sydney and had decided to take six months off to backpack around Europe. They were leaving for Munich the next day.

We sat there chit-chatting, smoking pot and what-not when Paul went ahead and cut to the chase and suggested that we continue the conversation at our hotel room. Nathan and Lucy looked at each other and smiled in agreement.

We started back to our hotel. We took the marijuana with us then we stopped at a little store and bought some beer. We went up to our room and talked and drank and smoked. As we sat on the bed, we exchanged stories and laughed. We also flirted a little back and forth with each other. Nothing too obvious, but there was a definite sexual attraction between us. A little while later, Nathan and Lucy started making out right in front of us. Paul leaned over and whispered. "See, I told you." We started making out too.

Nathan and Lucy were apparently old hands at couple swapping because they knew exactly what to do. While Paul and I made out, I suddenly felt another set of hands on me. It was Lucy. She looked me in the eyes and smiled and then pulled my head over to hers and began kissing me. It was my first time to be kissed like that from a woman. It was different to be sure. So much softer and sweeter than with a man. It felt good and seemed to awaken some new feelings in me. I was beginning to get really steamed up. Nathan continued rubbing her breasts and kissing her shoulders while we kissed. Paul did the same with me. It wasn't long before Lucy was taking my clothes off. I didn't have a problem with it and I started taking hers off as well. Nathan joined in and when Paul saw that he was the only one that was still dressed he took his clothes off too.

"Wow, he's big," Lucy said breathlessly as she took a look at Paul's cock. This really turned her on even further and she began to really kiss me then. Her hand was on my pussy and she began to rub my clit. "You're really wet," she murmured as she kissed my neck. "I can't wait to taste you," she said as she moved her hands all over me.

"I love your tits," she said. "They're so big and beautiful," she said as she began to suck my nipples. She was really turning me on. I had never realized that I could be so turned on by another woman but this was because I hadn't ever been with another woman. Sure, I had had fantasies but they were nothing like this. Mine were almost like I had been just inserting a woman into the man's role in sex. This was a completely different experience. It was so much more sensual that I could have ever imagined. This girl was making me so wet that I couldn't wait for her mouth to be between my legs. Her body was amazing, so tanned and muscular. Her breasts, while considerably smaller than mine, were firm and very well-shaped. They were perfect on her. This was one hot girl.

Pretty soon, I got my wish and she was between my legs and licking my pussy. She concentrated mainly on the clit but moved her tongue up and down the length of it, teasing me with it. Nathan was behind her eating her out. She moaned for him to start fucking her and he put it in, gently thrusting, so she could continue to lick me. I leaned over and began to suck Paul's dick. His erection was enormous so I knew that he liked what he saw. Lucy licked me good and sucked my clit like a pro. I came very fast, but she didn't stop. She licked me to another shuddering orgasm almost immediately after.

I knew then that I wanted to taste her. I had always tasted myself during sex so I wanted to see if tasting her was as big a turn-on for me. We switched. I went down on her and found out that it was even more of a thrill. She tasted good but different from me. My pussy was wet again. I motioned for Paul to come over and get behind me. I wanted him to fuck me while I licked the girl. He entered me easily and as he began to thrust against me, I was in heaven. I was hot and I knew that I was on my way to another orgasm. Between Paul's big cock filling me up and the taste of Lucy, I knew that I would have to come again. This orgasm came from deep within me and I couldn't help but be noisy with it. After I was finished, he then pulled out. I then felt another cock enter me. It was Nathan. He was pretty big but it was definitely different from Paul's. The difference only made me hornier.

I continued to eat Lucy's pussy and pretty soon she began to come. She was almost shrieking from the orgasm and I was so proud of myself making her come on my first time. After it subsided, she sat up.

"Now, I want to fuck him," she pointed at Paul. "I want that big cock."

She backed up to Paul and started rubbing up against him. He was still hard because he had yet to come. He entered her slowly. She gasped. "Oh, this thing feels so good!"

I have to admit that I felt a bit of jealousy come up when I saw him with her. However, I focused on the pleasure that I was getting from Nathan. I knew that everyone was just having a good time. No one was trying to do anything other than what was normal under the circumstances. I realized that jealousy was just an inconvenience that keeps us from truly enjoying ourselves sexually. I put it out of my mind and ground against Nathan even harder. He was really beginning to hit my g-spot.

Paul picked up the pace and took her breath away. Nathan did as well. This was the way I really liked it. Hard and fast.

It wasn't long before Lucy came again as did I. Nathan and Paul apparently couldn't handle it any more and both of them came right after that. Paul squirted all over Lucy's ass while Nathan shot his load on my breasts. He apparently had built up so much pressure from the night that some of it missed me and hit the wall behind me with a thud. We all collapsed on the bed and started laughing. It was pretty funny and great way to end the encounter. We smoked some more pot and drank some more beer before we went to sleep.

13

Nathan and Lucy left the next morning after eating breakfast with us at the hotel. But not before I had sex with Lucy again. I was glad that we had decided to let them stay the night. It was Paul's idea. He said that he felt bad that they had to go back to some crummy hostel. He said that they should spend at least one of their nights in Amsterdam in a nice hotel. They hadn't argued. The sex with Lucy was great again. Probably even better than the night before. It was just us this time. The guys just watched. It was like we were putting on a show for them. We were still a little pent up from the night before. Apparently we hadn't gotten enough of each other. We were all over each other, kissing and licking and grinding. I loved the way she tasted and I couldn't get enough of eating her out. She didn't have a problem with this. When we finally orgasmed by scissoring our legs together it was an astounding orgasm. Rubbing our pussies together like that was truly mindblowing. Paul and Nathan even applauded when we finished. We all laughed. While I still loved dick first and foremost, I knew that I would have to have another woman again. I was so grateful to Paul for letting this happen. If I had been with any other man, I know that there would have been nothing but resentment and weirdness because of it.

Over the next few days, we didn't really do that much. We rented a car and drove around the suburbs a bit. Paul showed me the place where he had lived with his aunt. It was a fairly non-descript house that was very typical of all the other houses in the area. She had moved back to Belgium a few years earlier so the place appeared to now be populated by a tow-headed Dutch family. A tall tow-headed Dutch family. I couldn't believe how tall everybody was. We also went to Delft and bought some porcelain which we had shipped to the States.

"It's something you're required to do when you're in the Netherlands," Paul said, matter of factly.

"Oh," I said.

"That and buying wooden shoes," he added.

He wasn't kidding. Well, maybe he was a little, but we did actually go and buy some. It was really fun and showed a real goofy streak in him that I hadn't seen before. All in all, we just did easy, low pressure stuff. Which was what vacations were for. We also had lots of sex. The encounter with the Australian couple had really sparked my libido so I was all over Paul whenever we made it back to the hotel.

Then, out of the blue, on the night before we left, Paul, announced that he wanted me to go out to the Red Light District and pick up no less than three college boys. He said that I had to bring them back to the room and fuck them. He put it just like that, "no less than three." This was it, I thought. He wanted me to get gangbanged.

"You need this, Elise. I know how much you loved having sex with multiple men. So I want you to do it again. This is a desire that you have and unless I tell you to do it, you will not have the courage. I want you to have fun. That's what this trip is about."

I was a little taken aback and started to say that I didn't really feel like it, but then I remembered that I had promised him. I also couldn't help but pick up on what he had said about me not having the courage to do it. He was right about that and I was only confirming what he had said. It was something that I would not do on my own. But then I remembered what I had done with the two sailors. I had had fun. I had loved the feeling of fucking both those guys. Two sets of hands on me and two dicks in me had been an amazing thing for me. Three or more would be even better. I began to get hot and I knew that I would be well served to do what he said. After all, his wish was my command. It was out of my hands, right?

"And what we will you do?" I said. "Will you join?"

"I'll be around, making sure you do it and that things are okay. And, no, I won't join. The guys you pick up will probably behave differently if I'm around. They will be uncomfortable. I want them to be all over you. I want you to experience all they have to offer. "

I couldn't help but smile a little mischievously. And I was sure that I saw him smile too.

I immediately took a shower and got ready. I put on my sexiest clothes and was out on the street in record time. I didn't want to waste time because I knew that the longer I waited the more likely I would be to chicken out. I tried to not even think about it. I could tell that all eyes were on me as I walked down the street towards the Red Light District. I was sure that most people thought that I probably worked there. This only turned me on more.

I walked around for about five minutes before I sighted my prey. I saw them through the window of a bar. It was four athletic looking young guys. One of them was wearing a soccer shirt. It was for an English team so I figured that they were most likely from there. When I walked in and sat down at their table, I knew that I had been right.

Even though they were a little drunk, they were a bit taken aback by my boldness, but I didn't care. I knew that I was going to get what I wanted. They were men after all. I asked them if they minded if I sat down and they said of course not. Dressed the way I was, no man would have refused me. I could feel myself getting horny at the anticipation of being with them.

We chitchatted for a few minutes. They introduced themselves, but I didn't even bother to pay attention to their names. They bought me a beer. I had been right about them. They were in college and were some sort of break. They had come to Amsterdam for the pot and the girls. Jackpot.

One thing led to another and before we knew it, we were back at my room fucking. Men were so easy, I thought. Especially young men. I could have been an axe-murderer for all they knew but just the thought that they were going to get fucked by me was enough for them to throw all caution to the wind.

I was out of my clothes as soon as we hit the room. I thought about Paul. I knew that he was somewhere, just in case things got out of hand. I had faith in him and this faith allowed me to let loose. It felt great to be nude in a room full of clothed people even if it was just for a few minutes. I pulled the first one's pants down and had his cock in my mouth soon thereafter. The others took off their clothes and stood around stroking themselves while they waited to be serviced. Their eager hands groped my tits and ass and I become more and more turned on as I watched them bringing themselves up to full erections. I loved to be felt up like that and I knew it was going to be even better than the time with the two sailors. They had good bodies and their cocks were big. Paul was right. This was going to be fun. It was something that I wanted to do. I could tell that they loved my big tits because all of them made a point of licking and occasionally bending down and sucking my nipples. I made the circuit of them, sucking their big hard cocks, bringing each one up to the point of coming before I went to then next one. Now it was ready for what I really wanted. To be fucked.

I bent over and they took the cue. One in front of me to suck and the other in back for me to fuck. Everybody had a turn. I was so horny. I went through them like a hot knife through butter. Each one pounded me hard the way I liked. I think it was the only way they knew how to fuck. There was no finesse or gentleness involved. This was just pure animal attraction. What they lacked in experience they made up for in enthusiasm and the first orgasm was upon me before I knew it. The fact that I didn't even bother to keep up with which one I was fucking only made it hotter. It was just one dick after another, truly anonymous sex. I came over and over again until I was satisfied that I had had my fill. I got down in the middle of them and sucked each and every one off, letting them blast their semen all over my face and breasts. I felt so dirty and so sexy. I couldn't wait to be fucked by Paul.

I hurried them out of the room after they were done. I lied and said my husband was coming back soon and they didn't want to get caught by him. This worked because they didn't want to linger. Still, they were quite polite and thanked me and asked could they call me again. I said that we were only in town for the night. After they had left, Paul came into the room a few minutes later.

"I was in the lobby. I saw them leave. How was it?"

Still naked and flushed from fucking, I smiled. "Isn't it obvious?"

He smiled. I jumped on him and fucked him more intensely than I had ever up to this point. It was probably the most primal intercourse we had ever had. We went at it so passionately I felt the earth move. It was that powerful.

· · · ·

We checked out of the hotel the next day and started for Belgium. Paul said that he wanted to visit some of his relatives there so he was in no big hurry.

"Why don't you get along with them?" I asked.

"No, I get along with them great," he said.

"Then what's the problem?"

He turned and stared at me for a second. "Elise, they're not like me. At least not most of them."

"What do you mean?"

He thought for a second. "Let me think of a way of putting this."

We drove in silence for a few seconds.

"They act like they're aristocrats."

"What's so bad about that?

"They think that everyone should treat them that way too."

"They stuck up?"

He laughed. "Yes, that's the phrase. I couldn't think of it."

"Well, if they're anything at all like you, then I'm sure they're all right," I said.

"Oh, they're not bad. Not all of them. I think you'll love my cousin, Carolina. We're going to a party at her house tomorrow night."

I was a little surprised. "But Paul! You should have said something. I don't have clothes for something like that."

"Relax. We'll take care of it when we get to Antwerp. There's lots of great stores there."

We small talked a little more, but the encounter with the Australians and the college boys kept going through my mind, along with what he had asked me to do in submitting to him. I'll confess that he had been right about me loving it, but still I felt I needed to talk with him about what was going on with our sex life.

"Paul, when you were having sex with that girl, Lucy, you looked like you were having a good time, but you weren't as into it as I was. Why? She was really hot."

"I know. She was a…how you say…real piece of ass."

I started laughing. Paul never talked that way.

He laughed too. "You're right. She was hot. And I did enjoy fucking her, but I enjoyed it more that you enjoyed it. The same thing goes for the English guys. It felt really good for me to let you have that pleasure. It makes me happy to know that you're getting to do stuff that you really want to do. Stuff that you would never dream of doing on your own. Stuff that really satisfies you sexually."

"But you satisfy me. It's you that I want to go home to. This is just for fun," I said.

"Of course, but fun is very satisfying."

"I know it is. That's why I want you to have these sexual experiences. I know that you won't if I don't make you participate in them. That is why I've taken that reponsibility from you. You don't have to make the decision to deny yourself. I've been through this before with my other girlfriend. I don't want to go down the same foolish road again."

Remembering my own feelings when I saw him fucking Lucy, I had to get something else off my chest. "Paul, do you ever feel jealous when I'm with someone else? I know I felt it a little when you were with Lucy."

"Of course, I do. It's unavoidable. But then I look at your face and see how happy you are and what a good time you're having and I get over it. I trust you and I know that you love me. I know that you're mine and I can easily put up with these feelings as long as I know that in your mind and your soul you're being faithful to me. Your body is yours to do with what you will. I am just happy that you choose to be with me."

"I really thank you for this, Paul. At first I didn't really understand what you were getting at, but now I think I am. It is very liberating to have that responsibility taken from me. To let you tell me when and who I can have sex with."

"Look at it this way, Elise. I would rather share you than lose you. And if I don't share you, I know that you will go away. I know that I awakened something in you and I take responsibility for it. You would never do the things you crave without feeling guilty about it. That is why I have to make you do them."

"So do you have more stuff in mind?" I asked and grinned. I knew he did.

"We haven't even gotten started yet."

14

Antwerp was much neater and prettier than I had anticipated. It was also a lot cleaner. Paul had said it was a beautiful city, but he had said it in a way that didn't sound like he was too enthused. I think it was because he had spent so much time there that he took it for granted. Also, it was where most of his family lived.

We quickly found our hotel. We then went to a nearby shop and for a snack ate a very messy pastry. Paul had insisted that I had to try one of the things. It was pretty good but hard to eat. He said that the place we got them from wasn't as good as the one next to the college. I had no idea what he was talking about but I took his word for it. After that we went to meet his uncle, Marc.

As we drove, and even though we had discussed it, it really began to sink in just exactly what our relationship was becoming. I couldn't help but think about what Paul had said about me and my sexuality. Instead of concentrating so much on the particulars of my sexual encounters, I began to focus on myself. I began to wonder what exactly was happening to me and what was I doing. Everything I had done, I had done willingly. Even though Paul had told me to do them, I had wanted these things to happen. It had been no coincidence that these had been the things that I had fantasized about before. It was still hard for me to believe that I had actually done them. I was going against everything I had been taught about how a lady should act. I really was acting like a slut. The strange thing that I didn't care. I loved it. I wanted people to know just how sexual I was. Paul had awakened me and now I was growing even more in love with him. I was even more turned on by

Paul than I had been before. This was why our sex was so intense after each of the encounters. I still wasn't sure if I understood it all yet.

After we settled into our hotel, we drove out to the docks. Paul said that his family's fortune had been built in shipping and that his Uncle Marc ran the business. He also said that his uncle was practically the only person from the family left in the firm. The rest just figuratively sat on the board of directors and collected their checks.

"Is it a very hard business?" I asked, wondering why nobody in the family still worked with the company.

"Not particularly. I think the situation says more about my uncle than the business," he said and chuckled.

I soon found out what he meant. We arrived and were ushered up to his uncle's office by the secretary. It was a very large company. I knew that Paul had come from money, but when I saw the actual size of the building, it was then that I fully comprehended the full scope of his family's fortune. I was amazed. While it wasn't what exactly I would call a skyscraper, it was pretty close.

As we waited outside at his uncle's office, Paul spoke to the secretary in Dutch. Occasionally, he would translate for me. However, I found that if I relaxed my mind, I could understand some of it due to the fact that some of the words that were similar to English. I had noticed that Paul mostly spoke Dutch in Antwerp whereas he had spoken English exclusively in Amsterdam. I later asked him if this was because people didn't speak English in Antwerp. He said that they could but didn't do it as much as in Amsterdam. Besides, it just seemed more right to speak Dutch there since it was home.

Right before we went in, we heard his uncle screaming at someone over the phone. Paul started laughing.

"What did he say?" I asked.

"He said, and I quote, 'He hoped they would get cancer in their testicles and that they hoped they found out it was curable only after they had gotten them cut off.'"

"That's awful."

"No, that's just my uncle."

A few seconds later we went in to meet him. I couldn't help but notice that Paul and he bore a striking resemblance. The only difference was that he looked like a bloated, mean, asshole version of Paul. Plus he had a walrus size mustache which made him seem comical and unpleasant-looking at the same time. He was so European looking not only in his demeanor but in also in his appearance. While in Amsterdam, people had mistaken Paul for an American, there was no way that this would ever happen with his Uncle Marc.

Immediately after we entered, he said something to Paul in Dutch and looked at me a little contemptuously.

"Uncle, this is Elise. She is a very special person in my life and I have brought her to Antwerp to meet my family."

Uncle Marc smiled at me and stared right at my cleavage. He made no attempt to hide what he was doing. He looked so much like Paul that it was a little unsettling.

"It's nice to meet you, Elise. I can see what Paul sees in you. You look like the type of woman that would make a man very happy for a short period of time."

Paul rolled his eyes.

"Thank you," I said, not quite knowing what to think. It had been a long time since I had been insulted so directly.

Uncle Marc then looked at Paul and said something in Dutch. He again looked very smug.

Paul answered him back in Dutch and smirked back. Uncle Marc answered him with a raised eyebrow.

At this, Uncle Marc smiled and bowed to me. "It was very nice to meet you, Elise. I hope you enjoy your stay in

Antwerp. Paul is a fine boy who doesn't come back home nearly enough."

I said goodbye and left.

On our way out, I remarked to Paul, "Well, he certainly not very nice."

"He's upset that I don't want to work here," Paul said. "He thinks that you're the distraction that's keeping me from coming back to Antwerp. Everybody else in my family is fairly useless Eurotrash. All they want to do is lounge around in Monaco and travel around on their yachts. I was supposed to come and let him groom me to take it over."

"Well, am I a distraction?" I asked a little suggestively as we walked to our car.

"Well, of course," he said smiling. "A beautiful and sexy distraction. Very worthwhile too. But it's not because of you that I won't work here."

"Well, what is it?"

"My uncle is an asshole."

. . . .

We did the touristy thing the next day, drinking beer and sightseeing. We went to the botanical garden and to the old Market Square. We let a stranger use our camera to take a picture with the statue of Peter Paul Rubens. We also saw the Cathedral nearby. Paul took me shopping on Schutterhofstraat and bought me the most wonderful dress for the party. He also bought me a pair of diamond earrings. He really went way out of his way to find the guy, too.

"You can't go where the touristy stuff is," he said. "Those guys are ripoff artists."

Everything he bought me was gorgeous. And I couldn't get over the diamonds. I couldn't wait to put everything on and when the time to get ready rolled around, I was more than ready to get the night started.

A Mercedes picked us up later that night. The driver took us to a very nice part of town which was filled with many restored old, expensive art nouveau type houses. As we drove to our destination, a neighborhood called Cogels Osylei, Paul leaned over and had almost a pained expression on his face.

"What is it?" I asked.

"I have a favor to ask. I know our relationship is rather an open one, but I want you to do something for me. I ask you rather than tell you, because I'm not sure how enjoyable this will be for you. I promised you that I would never make you to do something that you wouldn't like, but I'm not so sure about this."

"What is it?"

"My old roommate and friend from boarding school is going to be at the party. In fact, he is Carolina's ex-husband. He was always quite arrogant with me and never overlooked any opportunity to demean me when we were younger. Because he's a Count, he always acted very superior with me, even though my family has much more money his. He always acted like I was a peasant. I hated him."

I nodded. "But how can he be your friend if you hated him?"

"It's a European class thing," he explained. "We don't acquire friends the same way you Americans do. We are more or less assigned to many of them from birth. It's very advantageous for both of our families to remain connected. We also have no choice but to move in the same circles. Anyway, when he tries to seduce you…"

"What? When…?" It was a little much for me to take in on such short notice.

"Oh, I know Andre. When he sees you, I know that he will want you. Especially because you're with me. Even if he wasn't interested in you, he would do it just to spite me. But I know that he'll barely be able to keep his hands off you so I know that he'll make a pass at you. When he does this, go along with him. Have sex with him. Rock his world as they say, but when you're finished tell him how much better I am than he is. How my dick is bigger, etc... This will kill him."

I was still a little puzzled but all this, but since it was Paul, I was willing to go along. "A revenge fuck?" I asked, for clarification.

"In a matter of speaking. It would mean so much to me."

Without hesitation, I agreed. Paul was the man I loved after all. He had done so much for me, how could I turn him down?

Then the car stopped. We were there. The driver let us out and we walked to the door. After the servant took our coats, we were led into the main area of the house. There were many people there, mostly dressed fairly nicely. It wasn't a tuxedo-type affair, but it was dressy. The house also looked like something from a magazine. Or an old movie. We were greeted by Paul's cousin, Carolina. She was drinking wine. Another woman was with her.

"It's so nice to finally meet you, Elise. Paul has said so much about you."

Carolina was a gorgeous woman with very light hair. She was quite elegant but still extraordinarily casual. She acted like this kind of soiree was something she did every day. There was no family resemblance to Paul whatsoever. It was hard to think they were even related.

"Thank you. I've heard many good things about you as well."

She then introduced the woman who was with her. It was her girlfriend, Anna. I was surprised but tried not to show it. Paul hadn't said anything about Carolina being a lesbian. I would have to scold him about this later. I should have known something was up from the way that Anna was looking me over. She was definitely checking me out and the thought of her doing so made me a little turned on. She was an absolutely stunning woman, as was Carolina. However, she had a hardness about her that let me know that she was would probably be very dominant in bed.

"I want to apologize for my stepfather's actions today. He can be a real bastard at times."

"Your stepfather?" I asked.

"Marc is her stepfather," Paul explained.

"Yes, he married my mother when I was a teenager. Unfortunately."

That explained the lack of family resemblance.

"He's absolutely dreadful, but he's quite wealthy which seems to smooth over most of his personal shortcomings. At least it did for my mother," she added with a laugh.

We chitchatted for a while and then started mingling. We drank wine and talked. After a while, a good looking, but very oily guy with slicked back hair came up to us and smiled. I couldn't help but notice that his teeth were small, but perfectly straight. Almost rodentlike, I thought.

"Paul, it's so good to see you again." He then bowed to me and smiled in a way that let me know exactly what was on his mind. "And who is this lovely lady you have with you?"

Paul sighed and smiled. "Elise, this is Andre, my old friend and roommate."

I knew it. "The Count?" I asked just to play along with what was obviously a large ego.

Andre tut-tutted. "There's no need for titles, especially here at my ex-wife's party."

We small-talked for a bit and I have to say that at first, he didn't seem like that much of an asshole, but then his true nature slowly began to appear. At first, it showed up in some very snarky remarks he began to make about Carolina's sexual orientation. About how, after him, there was no man who could possibly satisfy her so she had been forced to turn lesbian. Even though he managed to hold that lecherous smile of his, it was a little uncomfortable due to the amount of spite that was in his voice. We changed the subject.

"So, Andre, what are you up to these days?" Paul asked.

"Not much. I'm still involved with my racing team but other than that, nothing much," he said.

"Andre owns an automobile racing team," Paul explained. "It's his pride and joy."

"I love it the way any father would love his children. Except mine have four wheels and go zoom zoom zoom," he chuckled. "How about you?" he asked Paul. "Still sitting with your little books and looking at your little numbers?"

Paul laughed uncomfortably. I now knew exactly what he was talking about regarding Andre being an asshole.

We talked for a bit more and then went to mingle some more.

A little while later, as Paul had predicted, I was approached by Andre.

"Elise, could you come back here with me?" He gestured with his wine glass down a hallway. "I have something I want to ask you." His smile was still in full effect.

He was so obvious. But I was more than ready so I didn't even bother to play hard to get. I was still a little horny from thinking about Carolina's girlfriend and was more than in a mood to help Paul. "Sure," I said.

He led me down a hallway to a bedroom. Of course, he closed the door behind him. He was so sure of himself; it made me a little sick.

"Elise, I was wondering… Most American girls have implants in their breasts, yes?"

"Some do."

"Well, I was wondering about yours? Yours are so beautiful, I thought that there's no way that they can be real."

I almost laughed at the clumsiness of his pickup attempt. However, I wanted to get this thing going so I thrust them out towards him. "Feel them and tell me what you think."

He grinned like a rat and began groping me. "Oh, yes," he said. "These have to be real."

I began to get turned on by his groping and I allowed him to keep pressing closer to me. He was a good looking guy after all; it was just his personality that was awful. I could have a good time with him as long as he kept his mouth shut. Besides, he was a Count. How often do you get to fuck a Count?

We began to kiss and we pressed our bodies against each other. His hands were all over my ass and I began to get really horny. I could feel his erection against me and I couldn't wait to suck it. I wanted to see exactly what I was dealing with. It felt big, but not as big as Paul's. I wanted to find out for sure. I got down on my knees and pulled his pants down and began to go down on him. His eyes rolled back in his head with delight and he smiled widely. "Oh, yes," he said as I sucked him. I continued until I could tell that he wasn't going to be able to take much more and then I pulled my skirt up and turned around and presented myself to him.

"Mmm...no panties..." he murmured as he took his hand and felt my waxed pussy. "And so smooth." He rubbed me and stuck his finger in. "Nice and wet, too." He then entered me with his dick and started gently thrusting against me, doggie style. I didn't want to look at him when he fucked me. I didn't want to invite any of his smarmy conversation. It was almost a galloping fuck, like he was riding a horse. It felt very unusual but still very good. Once I got used to the rhythm, I really got into it. Apparently he did too because, after a while, he ceased the gentleness and started giving it to me hard. I couldn't help but get into that.

Even with all his faults, I have to say that he was good. He pounded me and I came easily. I fucked him back hard as well. I ground against that dick of his and I could tell that he was in pure heaven. He was nowhere near as good as Paul or even the anonymous guys with whom I had had sex, but it wasn't because of what he was doing. It was his attitude. He fucked with an arrogance that made me feel a little used. He leaned over and rubbed my tits as he began to fuck me hard. I came again and decided that it was time to pull the plug. I bucked against him hard and he came shortly thereafter.

As we put on our clothes, he raved about how good I was and how he had never had sex with someone like me. He said that I was built for sex and that he would remember this for the rest of his life.

It had been good for me too, but it was definitely not the highlight of my life. His flattery almost led me to chicken out and not say anything bad to him. But his true nature eventually prevailed. He couldn't conceal himself for too long, even when he had been fucked so well.

"It's too bad that you're wasting your time with a stick in the mud like Paul. You need a real man who could fuck you the way you need to be fucked, who is worthy of your beauty and your sexual appetite. You need a man who knows what you need and is well-equipped enough to give it to you." He smiled and seemed to thrust out his chest in triumph, as though he had just told me something that would somehow change my life.

I stared at him and laughed. '

He laughed too, nervously. "What?" he asked.

"Paul is the best fuck I've ever had. He has the body of a god and his dick is huge. Bigger even than yours. You were good, Andre, but you're in not in the same league as Paul. Not by a long shot."

Andre's face fell. "Surely, you're joking. But Paul is…"

"No. Paul is so good that he should be paid for fucking. He should be in porn movies he's so good."

Andre's face fell. "Really? But I…"

"Sorry, Andre," I said and left. I couldn't stop smiling. It felt good that I had helped Paul get revenge and even better that I had been able to tell the truth in doing so.

15

After we left the party and had gotten back to our hotel, I filled Paul in on all the dirty details of what had gone on between Andre and I. I didn't leave out anything from the sucking to the fucking to me letting Andre know about Paul's superiority as a lover. He was so delighted.

"I would have loved to see his face," he said. "He is such an arrogant bastard that anytime he can get his comeuppance, it's usually well deserved."

"Well, he got it," I said.

"But was he good?" Paul asked, fishing for more information. It was then that I began to realize just how demoralized that he must have felt by Andre growing up.

This was so unlike him. He was so obvious about what he was trying to find out that it was almost a little sweet. I felt even better about helping him out.

"He was good, but it's not that sensual to feel like you're being fucked by someone's ego rather than their dick."

Paul looked at me as though I hadn't given him the answer he was looking for.

"Of course, he wasn't as good as you, Paul. I don't think it's possible to top you. You're the complete package. You've got the body and the skill to go with it. After fucking you, nothing else measures up," I said, telling him the truth. "Besides I love you and that makes all the difference in the world."

I could tell he was pleased with that answer. It was the one he had been waiting for.

"And that big cock of yours doesn't hurt things either," I said sassily and grabbing him by the crotch.

He laughed. I could also tell he was hard. I was still a little turned on from fucking Andre. I fingered myself and looked over and could see his erection sneaking up the top of his waistband. I couldn't keep my hands off him and pulled his dick from his pants. He was so hard he looked like he was about to burst. I could tell that he was aching to come. I wanted to give him relief so I began to suck him and I could taste the precum immediately. This turned me on to know that he was this turned on by me and what I had done with Andre. I rubbed my clit that much more firmly, only stopping to occasionally taste myself. I quickly had an orgasm and he soon followed, no doubt pushed over the edge by my moans. He came in my mouth and I was more than happy to swallow every drop. I licked that big dick of his until I had cleaned up every bit of his semen. We went to bed right after that and slept until morning.

••••

The next morning, I was filled with questions. This was such a strange new world I had found myself in that I simply had to know everything about it. I found out that Carolina had been practically been forced by her stepfather, Marc, into marrying Andre. According to Paul, she had always been very experimental with her sexuality but being with Andre had made her realize that she enjoyed the company of women more than men. Paul said that he had laughed out loud when he had found out that she had come out as a lesbian, knowing that Andre had gotten a comeuppance once again. Carolina hadn't wanted to marry him to begin with, but had just gone along to please her mother, who was only trying to please her stepfather, Marc. "He was the one with the pursestrings after all." After she came out, Marc forced her out of the country so she could not embarrass him by "cavorting with her dyke friends," as he liked to say. He said that he would not tolerate the scandal that her coming out would cause. Sure this was okay for Hollywood actors and degenerates, but not one of the wealthiest families in Belgium. He was so old fashioned that it was ridiculous. During this time, she had lived with Paul in the States.

"We had a great time. This was about five years ago," Paul said. "Eventually, Uncle Marc decided that enough time had lapsed for her not to be a disgrace any more and then he said she could go back to Antwerp."

"Does he really have that much power in your family?"

"Not really. Unless, of course, you're like most of the people in my family and don't work anywhere. He can make collecting on your trust difficult if he wants."

"So that is why you don't work for him?"

"Of course. Also, as you can tell, he's absolutely unbearable."

We went out to breakfast and did some more shopping. We also stopped by and visited with some more of Paul's relatives, another uncle and the aunt he had stayed with in Amsterdam. He was right; they did act a little haughty and aristocratic as well as a little old fashioned. It wasn't anything too bad though. In fact, I found it a little quaint. His aunt told me stories about him when he was a teenager. While were there, another cousin, Jeroen, dropped in with his wife, an extraordinarily overdone woman he called Miep. Her jewelry alone was enough to comment on. It was big, gold and so outrageous that it had to be real. She also had big hair, big boobs and an absolutely hot body. She would have been at home on a porno set, which according to Paul was where Jeroen was rumored to have met her. I was intrigued by her but didn't have enough time to get to know her. I tried to set up a lunch with them but they were going to Cannes the next day. All in all though it a nice little visit.

A little later, in the afternoon, Paul got a phone call. It was from his Uncle Marc. Apparently he wanted Paul to go to Hamburg with him that evening to have dinner with the owner of a company that he was potentially going to buy out. Even though he didn't want to, Paul agreed to go.

"It's hard to say no to him. Besides, I'm the only person in the family he trusts with business."

He would be gone until morning. In order for me not to be alone that night, he called Carolina and asked her if she could babysit me. It was easy to hear from her response that this was something she was definitely keen on. She said she would come by and pick me up later.

"Have fun, tonight," Paul said before leaving to meet his uncle. "Indulge her. You'll enjoy yourself, she's a fun girl."

"By indulge, do you mean fuck her?" I asked, wondering if this was another one of his assignments.

Paul smiled. "If you want. Just have fun. I'm sure she won't corrupt you too badly."

Then he left.

I missed him already but I was already excited at the prospect of a night out in Antwerp with Carolina. I figured that Anna would also be along. I took a nap and it was just getting dark when I woke up. I got ready and waited. A little while, her car showed up. I wasn't surprised to see that I had been right. It was both Carolina and Anna.

"Get in," Carolina said smiling. She was smoking a cigarette.

Anna smiled and moved over so I there would be room for all of us in the back of the car.

"I didn't know you smoked," I said to Carolina after the car started moving.

"I don't," she said, smiling. "I'm just smoking now."

"Oh."

After the usual pleasantries were exchanged, Carolina turned to me. "I was so glad when Paul called. It's always good to have people to join us on our little girls' nights out."

Anna chuckled.

"I'm glad to that you don't mind having me along." I said.

"I think Anna is happier than I am," Carolina said.

Anna smiled. "It's not everyday that you meet someone as sexy and beautiful as you, Elise."

I couldn't help but blush. She spoke with a very undiscernible accent. I couldn't quite figure out where it was from, but it was quite sexy.

"Any man or woman would be glad to be seen in public with you as company," she added.

Carolina winked at me.

"Thank you," I said, not knowing exactly what to say. I couldn't help but stare at Anna who was so hot and sexy that she was making me wet. I remembered the Australian girl and felt myself flush from the memory.

We went out for dinner in a quite hip part of Antwerp called the Zuid and then went for drinks. We talked and laughed and flirted. We had a lot of fun and Anna made no attempt to restrain herself from touching me every chance she got. Carolina was very sexy too, but a little more reserved. I could tell that she was very fond of Paul. I also found out that she and Anna had been together for a couple of years. Anna was from the Czech Republic and had once been a model.

After a while, we left the restaurant. Carolina instructed her driver in Dutch to go somewhere else.

"Where are we going now?" I asked.

"Somewhere I know you'll enjoy," Carolina said, smiling. Anna laughed too. We were all a little drunk at this point.

"Great," I said.

Carolina leaned in. "Paul told me about your relationship. About you and what you do."

I was speechless. "But…"

"Ssshh…It's okay," she said. "I love the fact that you're so free sexually. I think that if more people were like you, there would be fewer problems in the world. Paul is so excited about it that there's no way that I could possibly judge you."

"Yes, it's so hot," Anna added. "When Carolina told me, I had to get out my vibrator."

With that she and Carolina started giggling like a couple of school girls.

I didn't know what to think, but the thought of Anna masturbating was enough to send my thoughts about her into overdrive. And Carolina too. I felt myself really beginning to heat up.

"You're like sex walking," Carolina said, matter of factly. "It's only natural that you would have to fuck a lot. It's what you're made to do."

"We're going to the red light district," Anna blurted out, a little tipsily. "We're going to a sex show."

"Red light district?" I asked. "Like in Amsterdam?"

Carolina rolled her eyes. "Antwerp's red light district makes Amsterdam's look like Disney World. This is the real deal, baby."

"You don't see so many tourists here," Anna explained.

As we were driven into Antwerp's red light district, I could immediately see what she meant. It really was a sleazy place. It seemed a little unwelcoming, very unlike the one in Amsterdam. It was also a little scary, but she seemed to know what she was doing. The driver let us out in front of a house that was located just off the main street. We walked up and rang the bell. She spoke to the person on the other side in Dutch. The door was opened and we walked in.

The place was filled with people. Outside, it looked like just a house, but inside, it was a club. It was dark and what lights existed were either red or dim. It was obviously the kind of place where people wanted to remain anonymous. As we walked, I occasionally felt hands on my ass. I didn't mind, but it was a very surreal experience. The people who did make eye contact with me smiled. I smiled back but I didn't engage them any more than that. I followed Carolina and Anna through the place, through the common areas to one of the back rooms. It lit up in the center and was filled with people. I looked a little closer and I could see why. There in the middle of the room on a mattress was a muscular black man with a very large cock fucking a big-titted blonde-haired girl. She had a great body and seemed oblivious to the crowd that was watching her. They were really putting on a show and the sexual energy in the room was obvious.

"Look at that cock, Elise," Carolina murmured to me and put her arm around my waist. "How would you like to fuck that thing?"

I had to admit that I would have liked to fuck it very much. It looked even larger than Paul's. I strained my eyes to get a closer look.

"Anna loves black cock," she added, letting her hand slip down to my ass.

I looked over at Anna, who was absentmindedly rubbing her breasts as she watched. She nodded. "Black cock is wonderful."

"But I thought you were lesbians?" I asked beginning to feel the effects of Carolina's hands upon me.

"Sure, but sex is sex and orgasms are orgasms. My personal life is one thing, but my sex life is a little more open-minded," Carolina said, chuckling and leaning in and nuzzling my neck. Anna joined me on the other side and pretty soon we were all standing close together, rubbing our bodies together as we watched the show.

I couldn't help but get hotter and hotter as I watched the fucking that was going on in front of me. People in the audience were groping each other and masturbating. Some just stood there watching and smoking cigarettes. The more I watched, the more I realized that I wanted to be the girl who everyone was watching. I realized that this kind of attention was what I was always seeking when I was having sex with other people. It was what fueled my sex drive. The couple were really going at it now, fucking hard against each other. I reached down and pulled my skirt up, but before I could put my hand to my pussy, Carolina put hers there instead. She moved behind me and kissed my neck while rubbing my clit. I ground against her hand. Anna divided her attention between us and the couple having sex. She moved in and started kissing my neck again. I was in heaven. If the Australian girl had been good, this was great. Just like with men, if one was good, then two were better. These were women who knew their way around a woman, too. They were so horny it was obvious where this was going.

"Let's go back to my house," Carolina said breathlessly. "You can't get too carried away in a place like this or you have to beat back the crowd."

As the couple continued to have sex, we left and took the car back to her house. We were all over each other on the way there, groping and kissing. Anna licked my pussy while Carolina kissed my neck and sucked my nipples. After we got back to her place, we were barely in the door before we were at each other again. The house was so beautiful that it only enhanced the experience. Such a setting was always sensual. Just being in Europe was exciting, but to be in a house like this was beyond thrilling. We couldn't get enough of each other's hands, mouths and pussies. It was as though we were all so horny that we didn't want to disconnect from each other. Somehow or another we made it to the bedroom and were soon a writhing mass of flesh, working towards our pleasure. The place was beautiful and decorated wonderfully in a very art nouveau way that completely matched the exterior. If I hadn't been so horny, I would have just admired the beauty of it, but I had other things to take care of first. Things I needed to do. I couldn't wait to start eating Anna's pussy. She was ready for me and ground her juicy wet lips against my face as I brought her to orgasm while Carolina licked me. Their skin and lips were so soft that it was just a uniquely arousing experience. Their tastes were wonderful and unique and their orgasms were also different. Carolina was forceful and loud when she came while Anna whimpered a little. It was just so hot and I was so happy that

I was getting to experience sex like this. Expecially in such a setting. After much mutual groping and licking, Anna maneuvered me into a position where our pussies were scissored against each other. It was the same position that I had been in with Lucy, the Australian. I had loved that position with her and I could tell that Anna was going to work me over good. She fucked me like that, grinding that wet pussy against mine until I came. Then she ground against me some more until we both came. I switched out and Carolina took my place and I fingered myself as I watched them both have the biggest orgasms of the night. I guess seeing each other with me had had the same effect on them as seeing me with other men had on Paul.

After they finished, Carolina looked over at me. "Next time, we'll break out the dildos."

We all cracked up.

After we composed ourselves, still nude we went downstairs and had some drinks. We talked about the time we had just had and relived some of the best moments. I told them how wonderful they were and just how turned on they had made me. I know I was gushing but it was just that great of an experience for me.

"After tonight, you probably think our whole family is depraved, right Elise?" Carolina said, joking.

"Oh, no, "I said.

"Well, we are," she said and laughed. "But in a good way."

"I'll say," I said and laughed.

A little while later, Carolina turned to me and said very seriously, "Whatever you do, Elise. Don't change."

"What do you mean?" I asked.

"Don't become ashamed of what you are or what you do sexually."

"I'm not sure what you mean."

"I mean that sometime in the future when you start having regrets and start feeling ashamed about being so open sexually, put them quickly out of your head. Have no regrets. Do not listen when other people talk about you. They are not you and they do not know your needs and desires. Ignore anyone who criticizes you and your choices. If you do not do this, you'll not only drag yourself down, but also Paul. Enjoy yourself and you'll always be happy."

"I'll try to remember that," I said, pondering the words.

"It's the only way to live life and be happy. If you don't accept what you are, then you'll be miserable. So many people never learn this."

She paused for a second as if she was considering saying something else. She took a sip of her drink. "You're very lucky, Elise. It is so much easier to be open sexually when you have someone who loves you. If you were out on your own, there would be so many more emotions that you would never truly be happy."

"What do you mean?" I asked.

"When you're single and having sex with lots of men and women, you're always wondering if they love you. If they'll call back. If you'll ever hear from them again. But when you're with someone who loves you, you don't have to worry about these things. You just concentrate on the sex because you know when you go home, there will be the person who loves you. It took me many years to figure this out. Right, Anna?

Anna raised her glass as if she was toasting in the affirmative.

We drank some more and I thought about her words. I knew that she was right and I was glad that I had had the opportunity to meet her.

Then we broke out the dildos.

16

Paul arrived back from Hamburg the next day as scheduled. We visited some more of his relatives and hung out with Carolina and Anna some more. A few days later, we went back to the States. Of course, I had told Paul all about my time with them. He immediately started laughing.

"She's tried to sleep with every girlfriend I've ever had. Now she's finally succeeded!"

We both laughed.

On the flight back, Paul fulfilled his promise to join the mile high club with me. We waited until everyone was asleep and then I gave him a hand job under his blanket to get him good and hard. I, of course, was already wet. It was fairly obvious what was going on when we got out of our seats. Paul's erection was so large it almost stuck out like a separate limb from his body. I could almost swear that I saw the flight attendant smile when we left our seats. However, she turned her back to us so I'm not sure. Maybe she was just giving us a little privacy. I'm sure that couples did this all the time. We went to the restroom and fucked like mad. It was a quickie but it was hot. Luckily we both managed to come quickly so we didn't have to worry about someone trying to get into the bathroom on us. It was uncomfortable though, I ended up getting a leg cramp from the experience. I then realized that the big deal in joining the mile high club wasn't necessarily because it was hot but also because it was so hard to do.

After we arrived back in the States, we pretty much settled into our routine. Both us went back to work. We saw each other a little bit but there was so much to catch up on that it was difficult. Still, we managed to sneak in some sex here and there. Paul didn't give me any assignments, but then again I didn't need any. I had too much going on at work to think about sex. Besides, our European vacation had helped fulfill so many fantasies, I figured I was good for a while.

However, my mind kept going back to what Carolina had said. It had really hit home just how lucky I was. Most men would not have allowed me to do what I was so compelled to do sexually. Most men wouldn't have understood. They would have used it as a reason to leave. Even my ex-husband, Eric, who didn't even act like I existed for the latter part of our marriage, would have eagerly jumped at the excuse to play hurt and leave me.

Paul was indeed special. He was strong and he was mine. I was so happy. I was such a better person for meeting him and being with him. Through him I had learned that sex is simply too good and too fun to confine to just one person.

Sometimes, however, I wondered what I would do if he wanted to be like me. If he wanted to be so sexual. I realized that I would have much more of a problem than he did. However, I also knew from his example that I would get through it. Besides, I had come to realize that this was not really his thing. If it was, he would be doing it. I realized that he could probably have any woman he wanted. He was so handsome, sophisticated and kind. He also had the European thing going which was always a plus with women. Women definitely liked him and he could have had his pick. Especially if they ever saw him nude. However, he chose to indulge me. I realized that this factor alone was like I had won the lottery.

About mid-week, Doreen and I went to lunch. We had seen each other briefly after I had gotten back in town but had been unable to talk due the large stack of work on my desk. After I had finally gotten it down to a manageable

102

level, I was able to go out. We met at the deli as usual. I knew she wanted to know about my trip. Every single juicy detail. However, I knew that I wasn't going to be able to tell her everything. At least not yet.

"So how was it?" Doreen asked, sipping an iced tea.

"It was great." I went on into detail about what we had done and my impressions of his family or at least the ones I had met.

Doreen just sat back and sighed. "This is so exciting. I wish Tom had an exotic background like that."

"Isn't Michigan exotic enough for you? That's what you always say anyway."

She laughed. "No, I said that it was like a foreign country to me. I mean Ann Arbor is nice, but I don't think it quite compares to Amsterdam."

I laughed too.

She paused and looked me over. "You have really changed since you met him, Elise. You're so much more lively and bright. Also, you're a lot sexier. I can tell that you're so happy. You really deserve it too. After what that asshole Eric did to you."

I nodded. "He was an asshole. But I'm glad he's gone. If he hadn't cheated on me, I wouldn't have Paul."

"Amen, sister," Doreen said. "Everything has a purpose even when your ex-husband is a complete bastard."

I couldn't help but laugh.

We ate some more. However, a weird thing started happening as we ate. Every man in the place would check me out when they walked past me. Some of them were really obvious about it too. They were checking Doreen and her big fake boobs out too, but it was nothing compared to the way they were ogling me. While this had happened sometimes before I had met Paul, now it was happening a lot. Today especially. It was probably my sexy clothes, but I think that I was also putting out some sort of vibe due to the all the sex I was having and context in which I was having it. It was like putting out a signal that I was open for business and all these guys were doing a little window shopping. I suppose that once it's turned on, you can't shut it off so easily. It just keeps transmitting all the time. It was a little strange, but also quite flattering. And very exciting. If Doreen hadn't been there, I'm sure I would have taken one of them back to the ladies room and made his day. I'm sure that Paul wouldn't have minded.

After a while, Doreen started chuckling and shaking her head.

"What is it?" I asked.

"Every man here is looking at you like you're a piece of meat."

"Are they?" I asked, pretending I didn't know what was going on.

"It's even making me hot," she said and pretended to fan herself. "Whatever it is that Paul's giving you, I need some of it."

I smiled, but didn't say anything about why people were acting the way they were towards me. I knew she was dying to know my secret so that she could get some of it for herself, but I knew that Tom wouldn't be able to handle it.

17

Then one day…

"You're ready," he said.

I looked at Paul and wondered what he was talking about. It had been a couple of months since we had gotten back from Europe. He hadn't given me any assignments and

I have to admit that I was starting to feel the urge to fuck. We had had great sex, but just reliving some of my "greatest hits up to now" was making me want to go and do *something*. I hoped that he had something in mind for me so I could get some relief. We had just gotten in from buying few groceries to prepare a little dinner at home when he said it.

"You did me a favor and helped me get revenge. Now I'm going to do the same for you."

"What do you mean?"

"I will help you steal Ginger away from your ex-husband."

"What?" I tried to wrap my mind around what he had just said. "What are you talking about?"

"You're going to pick her up and we're going to have a threesome with her. We'll screw her brains out in a way she has never had done before and any experience she has with your husband will never be able to measure up afterwards."

"But I don't want to do that. I've never even thought of it."

He shook his head. "Of course you do. You even said so yourself. You said that you wished that you had taken him up on his offer of a threesome and taken her from him. So, why wouldn't you want to do it now that you can? Besides I want you to. He was quite cruel to you when he called you. It's the only way you'll ever get closure. Real closure."

"But I have you. Isn't that closure enough?"

"No. What we have is a relationship. It's not the same as closure. Sure it will help you move on, but this will always remain a sorespot with you. This is why you need to have the last word and in a case like this your closure will be even greater if you can get a little revenge. Don't you want to stick it to your ex-husband in a way that he never dreamed possible?"

I had to admit it was an appealing idea but that subject was still a little raw for me. Thinking about catching him cheating with her still made me hurt.

"But I don't want to reopen any old wounds," I said. "I just want to get it out of my mind."

Paul looked at me squarely. "Elise, do you think for a moment that your ex-husband has ever regretted cheating on you?"

I had to admit no.

"Well, then don't you think that he should regret his new girlfriend cheating on him? This is your opportunity."

It did sound good. Still I had reservations. "But I still don't think so."

He shook his head. "It doesn't matter. I have decided it. I want this for you. You will thank me later. Besides didn't you say that she was your type?"

"So you're giving me no choice?"

"No. Consider it your next assignment."

. . . .

It was amazing how easy it was.

I found out Ginger's number and called her up and asked if she would like to meet for lunch. Amazingly, she said yes. She almost seemed happy to speak to me. It would be the first time we exchanged words. Other than me screaming at her when I had caught her with my ex-husband, I had never had a conversation with her.

I met her at a little place near Paul's apartment. I was early, but she arrived just a little after me. I waved her over. She was dressed to the nines and had apparently just come from work. I seemed to remember that she was involved in sales of some sort. I couldn't remember. Regardless, sitting across from her, I truly realized how beautiful she was. She

106

may have stolen my husband, but I couldn't take this away from her. She looked good. With her big boobs, blonde hair and thin body, she really was my type. My type before I had become so open sexually. Every woman has one, a type of woman that they think is beautiful and that they would make a same-sex exception for. Ginger made me tingle she was so sexy. Even though I was going to have to get through a whole lot of awkwardness here at the beginning, it wasn't going to be hard to put Paul's plan into action. At least not when we got going.

"I am so happy you called," she said, smiling. "I know that Eric invited you to our wedding. I thought that it might be a little forward but he was adamant."

"Yes, Eric is like that."

She laughed. "He is, isn't he?"

We chitchatted a little more. After our drinks came and we became more relaxed, I began to realize that I kind of liked her. She didn't seem to be at all the horrible person I had imagined her to be. Even though I didn't prod her or say too much, she seemed to find the same faults in Eric as I had. She was very forthcoming about how she thought he was selfish, immature and inconsiderate. She said it in a nice way though and I couldn't help but enjoy the conversation. Also as the alcohol started flowing, I began to get more and more steamed up for her. I couldn't help but begin to fidget in my seat, crossing and uncrossing my legs in anticipation of what we would be doing later. I couldn't help but notice how nice her tits were. I was sure they were fake, but I figured that I would find out for sure later so there was not point in asking. I had no doubt that I would be able to get her into bed.

We ate and drank and drank some more. She became very gushingly complimentary and apologetic the more she drank. She was in a very good place with the alcohol. A very pleasant drunk. I liked that.

"I'm so sorry about the way things happened," she said. "I didn't even know he was married. He told me that you two were separated."

"That's not surprising," I said. It definitely sounded like something he would say.

"I mean, after you caught us and the truth came out, I almost broke up with him. I couldn't believe that he would put me in a situation like that."

"Well, I can." I said.

We both laughed.

"But he sweet talked me back. You know the way he does? He just kept on and on until after a while, I just got tired of hearing it and decided to take him back."

I knew exactly what she was talking about. He was persistent that was for sure. Especially when he was trying to weasel out of something or, in this case get his way back into it.

We talked about our jobs and where we had gone to college. Eventually, I knew that it was now or never so I got up my courage. It would be my first time picking up a girl.

"My boyfriend's apartment is pretty close. Do you want to come up and have a drink there?

Her eyes lit up. "Of course."

. . . .

At Paul's apartment, I poured her a glass of wine. I sat beside her on the couch and we talked for a bit. Paul and I had decided on his apartment because it was nice and also because there was more room for a threesome. I took a large gulp of wine to get up my courage and when we had a moment where we were looking into each other's eyes, I leaned in and kissed her. Oddly enough she wasn't surprised. She kissed me back and started giggling.

"I love kissing girls," she whispered. "Ssssh. Don't tell Eric. He gets jealous."

"I don't intend on talking to him ever again," I said dryly and kissed her again.

For some reason this cracked her up. But what she had said about him was true and I knew exactly what she was talking about. Eric was the type of guy who fantasizes about his girl being with another girl but if she actually did it, he would sit in the corner and pout. Remembering this about him, made me feel even better about what I was doing.

We started kissing in earnest then. She was very aggressive and she went right for my boobs. She was all over them. "I love your breasts," she whispered as she sucked my neck. Her other hand went to my pussy and she was pleased that I wasn't wearing any panties. She wasn't wearing any either. I was getting wetter by the second but she was definitely in control of the situation. I began to wonder was I the only woman who was only recently bi? It seemed like every woman I was with was an old pro at this. I realized that I must have really missed the boat when I was younger.

We were out of our clothes in seconds and went at each other hard, groping and sucking each other breasts and rubbing our bodies together. I found out that she did indeed have fake breasts, but they were nicely done and extraordinarily hot. I couldn't get enough of her. I couldn't believe how turned on I was by her. I wanted to taste her and it wasn't long before I spread her legs and got down between them and started licking her pussy. I loved the way she tasted. She was very wet and once I started fingering her clit while I licked her, she came. After she finished, she was in between my legs and eating me. She was so good that she took my breath away. She wasn't gentle at all. She attacked it, like she had a lust for it that had to be sated immediately. I loved this approach and it was a little different from what I had experienced with the other women I had been with. Her aggression was a big turn-on and my orgasm was on me before I knew it. After I came, she locked our legs and rubbed our pussies together, humping each other. I loved this position and was glad that she had gone for it. If she hadn't I was going to. She was good. For a second, I wondered how life would have been different had I joined she and my husband in a threesome. She was experienced and knew exactly what to do to make me come. The fact that she was gorgeous too didn't hurt things.

But then, as planned, before she had a chance to come again, Paul walked in. He stood there watching and smiling for a second. Ginger didn't seem to mind and kept grinding against me, staring both he and I in the eye.

"Ginger, this is Paul, my boyfriend," I said breathlessly, still grinding against her pussy and trying to come again.

"Hello," she said so close to orgasm that she couldn't pull herself away from me. Paul and I had made sure that this would be the point at which he walked in, when she was so close to orgasm that jumping up and running away would not be an option.

"Mind if I join?" he said, not giving her a chance to answer before he pulled down his pants, exposing his massive rock hard erection.

As expected, her eyes almost popped out of her head. "Not at all," she said eagerly and humped me a little more forcefully. She didn't even hesitate. She didn't act as though she had any thoughts of Eric at all. This was working out even better than planned.

Paul undressed the rest of the way, and her eyes were all over him. I was proud of him and how he looked but also I felt a little bad about what were doing to her. I thought it was a little underhanded doing this to her relationship. But then again, I realized that if she was the type of girl who liked a little extracurricular sexual activity outside her relationship, then Eric should learn to live with it. After all, if a man can't accept a woman's sexuality then he isn't the right one for her.

Ginger and I disengaged ourselves from each other. Paul got between us and started kissing me first. Ginger leaned in and started sucking his cock right off the bat. Like most women, she was hungry for it. I leaned in and sucked some too. There was room for both us on either side of it. Occasionally, he would give me a look that conveyed the idea that the plan was working out great. After a little while of sucking him, he put both of us on our backs side by side on the couch and started eating us out. He would switch from one to the other, bringing us to the point of orgasm and then switching. It was very hot. Ginger and I kissed each other and played with each other's breasts while he was licking us. He then started fucking me. He pushed that big dick into me and started pounding me hard right off the bat. He didn't even take the time to enter me slowly. He must have been that turned on by the situation. Ginger was sucking my tits and rubbing my body as he pounded me. He filled me completely and hit my g-spot pretty quickly. I came so hard I quivered. Then he switched to Ginger.

She was ready for it. She giggled and pushed him back on the couch and climbed on top of him. She was going to ride him. "Ahhh," she said as his dick went into her. "Now that hits the spot." Then she started fucking him. I watched as she writhed on him, grinding her pussy against his big dick. It was hot and I started masturbating just watching them. She rode him hard and was loud about it, moaning and talking while she fucked him.

However, as I watched I couldn't help but feel little weird about it. I began to get a little jealous. She was just too familiar with him, I thought. She was being greedy with him. It was like she wanted him all to herself and was just waiting for me to get out of the way. And he was going along with it.

I pushed these thoughts out of my mind. They were stupid. She was just a sexually open woman like me. I should have looked at her as a kindred spirit not a rival. I tried to clear my head.

But then they started again. No matter how hard I tried to push the bad thoughts out of my head, I found that I was actually getting very angry with her. Not just her but also with Paul. He was really fucking her and he was enjoying it. I began to see red.

What was wrong with me? Paul let me do anything I wanted. I could have sex with anyone. Paul loved me so why was I feeling this way?

Then I realized what it was. Watching them together reminded of what had happened with her and my ex-husband.

"Oh, baby, fuck me hard!" she yelled, interrupting my thoughts.

That was it. Even though I had been able to rationalize what was happening and why I was getting upset, this really pissed me off. How dare she? How dare she call my boyfriend, "baby?" And worse yet, he was going along with it. I didn't care what kind of relationship we were in, there were lines that shouldn't be crossed. Sex was sex, but both of them were going too far. This wasn't going to happen to me again.

However, not wanting to be a wetblanket I sat back and seethed at them while they finished. When they eventually did.

They stayed in that position, fucking like animals until she started shrieking and shaking with orgasm. She acted like she was possessed and I couldn't help but feel disgusted at her. Paul came just a few seconds later.

"Wow, I've never had an orgasm like that!" she said, smiling at me. Like nothing was wrong.

"Good for you," I said.

We put on our clothes and chatted afterwards for a little bit. I faked my way through the small talk afterwards and pretty soon she left.

"Well, that went well," Paul said and put his arm around me. "Just wait until she tells Eric."

I looked at him and shook my head.

"What?" he said.

"This is what," I said and slapped him. Then I left the apartment.

18

I walked out of Paul's building and caught a taxi before he had a chance to catch up with me. I was so angry I couldn't stand it. I held my tears until I made it back to my apartment. After I got there I broke down. It was then that all the pain and disapointment I had felt at the breakup of my marriage came gushing out. I thought I had worked through all of this after my breakup but apparently I hadn't. Seeing Paul with the girl with whom my husband had cheated simply brought it all back. It brought back all the feelings of failure and resentment. All the feelings of disappointment and rejection. Everything that I hadn't properly dealt with.

Of course, there was a message from Paul on the machine as soon as I got back to my place, but I ignored it. I was too busy breaking down to listen to it. Besides, even though I knew it was misplaced anger, I was still mad at him. I couldn't help it. Even though I was now this open, sexually liberated person, I was still a human. I was still a woman. It didn't matter how much I could let myself go sexually, I could still get my feelings hurt.

A couple of days went by and he continued to call. I continued to ignore him. He came over and knocked on my door and tried to get me to talk to him, but I pretended I wasn't there. He came to my work, but I had security tell him I didn't want to talk to him. It was true that I was slowly getting over what had happened, but it still hurt. The thought of him fucking her kept going through my mind. It just kept reminding me of seeing Ginger and my ex-husband together. In my mind, I also kept hearing her saying, "Oh, baby." This didn't help things at all.

Damn her, I thought. Even, deep down, I knew it wasn't seeing her fucking Paul that I was upset about. I was upset that my relationship with Eric had ended the way it had. We had started out so young and so hopeful and it had all went to hell. We had let it die. Sure, it was probably over before it started, but it hurt to be a failure. And that's what I felt like. A failure. Seeing Ginger fucking Paul only reminded me of it.

Perhaps I was also becoming a little ashamed at what I had been doing. Maybe my upbringing and the conventional world's view of sexuality and morality was beginning weigh on me and my sexual escapades. Maybe being with Ginger and Paul had also awakened feelings of embarrassment. That I was doing wrong. It could have even been that I was jealous of the fact that Ginger was so sexually aggressive Maybe she was stealing some of my thunder?

A few days more went by and Paul kept calling. However, as I thought more and more about my situation, I slowly began to get some perspective. I knew that I wasn't angry at Paul or even Ginger. It wasn't their fault. It was just sex. I had been a sucker and had made it more than what it was. Sex was supposed to be fun. Expecially spontaneous sex like that. What had been wrong with me?

On my way home from work one day, it finally hit me just how stupid I was and what I was throwing away by being angry with Paul. Here was the man who had freed me. Who had opened up my world and I was throwing it away over some stupid little girl jealousy. I also remembered what Carolina had said about regrets and how I should never be ashamed of who I was and what I desired. She was right. I realized that my time of mourning was over. It was time to grow up. I was going to call him and explain myself and hope that he understood.

I rushed home to my apartment. Of course, there was the usual message from Paul, but there was also another one. It was from Eric, my ex-husband.

"What the hell have you done to Ginger?" he screamed. "She's some kind of sex maniac now. She's wanting to have threesomes and is talking about your boyfriend's dick. What did you do to her? Did you do this just to get back at me?" Blah blah blah. It went on and on and on. Just like that.

I started laughing. It was like a weight had been lifted off my head. I had been really stupid. Paul had been right. Revenge felt good. I did feel like I had had the final word. Now I had closure. I picked up the phone and called Paul.

"You were right. I'm sorry. I was stupid," I said before he had the chance to say anyting.

"That's okay. We all get a little upset sometimes," he said.

115

We talked a little more. Everything was okay now. He understood completely.

As I left to meet him, my phone rang. Thinking it was Eric, I let it ring. It wasn't. It was Ginger. She wanted to hook up with me again. Just me. She said that she couldn't get fucking me out of her mind.

I couldn't help but smile.

19

After Paul and I had reconciled, we had sex like crazy. We were insatiable for each other. Paul hadn't taken any offense to what had happened. In fact, he said that he had expected it in a way. He said that it was only natural that I would have these feelings and it was good that I was able to finally get over the hurt of my breakup. He said that he knew that I would eventually be okay but he had hoped it was sooner rather than later. He had been elated to get my call.

Everything was great and we had fun making up for the time we weren't together, but it wasn't long before I started getting the itch again. It was time for another assignment. Paul could tell that I was getting the urge for more when he came up with the idea for me to shoot a porno. I was a little nervous at first about having my face and body all over the internet, but I figured what the hell. It was who I was, so why not? Why be ashamed of something that I enjoyed? That was so much a part of me? Or better yet, what made me happy? Besides Paul told me to do it. At this point in our relationship, I had decided to no longer question him. I knew I would enjoy it.

He had to work the day I was supposed to film the movie so I had gone alone to a nondescript looking little storefront out in the suburbs. Once inside, I was surprised to see just how professional it all was. I had always thought stuff like this was done in the backroom of someone's house, but this was rather well-appointed for such things. I was dressed in a very short skirt and low cut top. My breasts were popping out and if I bent over you could see everything. My high heels just made everything that much more sexy. I loved the way I looked. I was dressed even more suggestively than I usually did. I liked it and knew that I would be dressing like this more often.

I was introduced to the photographer and then the videographer. As expected, they were both middle aged guys with beards, wearing comfortable shoes. I was then introduced to the guys I was going to be shooting with. They were two, young heavily tattooed muscular guys. A blond one and a brown-haired one. They were rugged looking, but very cute and probably in their early twenties. I could tell by the way they filled out their pants that they were both hung. This was going to be nice, I thought. Paul knew how much I liked sex with multiple men so I was glad that he had set up this particular kind of shoot. They smiled and I could tell from the way that they looked me over that they liked what they saw. After some small talk to get us acquainted with each other, the videographer said that they were ready to start shooting.

"I'm not really going to direct you, just do what comes naturally," he said, smiling. "I'll tell you if I need you to move so I can get a better shot."

We went over to a couch, one guy on either side of me. It was a little weird at first, sitting there in front of a camera and lights while someone waited on you to start fucking. It was a little forced and almost made me want to just say to hell with it and leave. However, these guys were too hot to pass up. After a few seconds of getting accustomed to the situation however, I knew that I would be okay. I just had to concentrate on their bodies and what they were going to do to me. I wanted to just pull off my clothes and start fucking. I wanted to wrap my arms and legs around their firm muscular bodies and get down to it but thought that we would probably need a little build up before we started. We sat around for a few seconds uncomfortably and I asked them if they worked out. It was obvious that they did and they almost laughed. They were immediately at ease. In reality, I should have been the nervous one here, but I wasn't. It was like I was the old pro and these two guys were the novices by the way they were acting. I could tell they could wait to put their hands all over me but were too gentlemanly to make the first move. Young guys were always so impatient. But I was too. I was ready to get fucked. I wanted to see what these two could do. I put my hand on the blond one's leg to let him know it was okay. This was all it took because his hands went directly to my breasts and the brown-haired one started kissing my neck and pulled my skirt up. His hand was on my pussy and I could tell that the fact that I was already wet turned him on. I put my hand on his crotch and could feel his dick grow even larger. He was a big boy that was for sure. His bulge hadn't lied. I couldn't wait to get that thing inside me. The brown-haired one already had his dick out and was stroking it, obviously waiting for me to start sucking it. It was also a big one. These guys were definitely the men for the job.

I started sucking the blond one's cock and pulled off my clothes. The brown-haired one did the same and I bent over so he could start fucking me. I needed him to start fucking me. I needed him to start pounding me. I needed an orgasm.

He didn't disappoint. He started out slightly easy so he could get that big thing in me, but as soon as he was comfortable, he started going to work. I had wanted to tell him not to bother that I could take it, but I thought it might have messed up the shot. But I soon got what I wanted. He started fucking me hard. Just the way I liked it. I couldn't help but orgasm almost immediately. I continued sucking the blond one and when I started tasting the precum I backed off.

"Let's switch," I said.

And they did. I could taste myself on the brown-haired one's dick. This really did it for me, tasting myself. I knew that I was going to orgasm again. I came once more on the blond guy's cock.

We switched around a few more times, fucking and sucking until they were about to come.

Finally the videographer said, "We've got enough footage, go ahead and come if you want."

I was a little startled as were the guys because we had completely forgotten we were shooting a movie.

When he said this, I was in the middle of fucking the brown-haired one again and sucking the blond one. They were both about to pop so I decided that I would be merciful and let them come. However, I could have fucked like that all day. I got down on both knees and started sucking and stroking them. It didn't take long for them to blast all over my breasts and face.

The videographer gave me a check for my work and I left immediately and went straight to the bank. I didn't even take time to clean up. I knew I still had that freshly fucked look and was still glowing from the orgasms I had just experienced just moments earlier. However, Paul had said that I needed to go the bank and cash the check as soon as possible. I needed to do it before it bounced. "You can't trust these guys when it comes to money," he said. He paused for a second. "Or anything else, for that matter," he added with a laugh.

Of course, he was right. He always was. And it wasn't even like the check really meant that much. It was just what it represented. That I had done something great. He didn't want me to get cheated out of any part of the experience. Besides it was a turn-on walking around like that. Had Paul intended that as part of the assignment? I hoped so.

• • • •

I hurried out of the bank and back to over to Paul's place. I was still horny as hell from the photo shoot. I just felt so sexually alive that I was walking on air. I was really looking forward to some good sex from him because I was still turned on. However when I got there, Paul had a very thoughtful expression on his face. I could tell something was going on.

"Is something wrong?" I asked.

"Oh, it's nothing. It's just that I am going to have to go to Antwerp for a few months. Maybe more. I have to take over the business. At least for a while anyway."

"Why? Is your uncle making you?"

"No, he's sick. His doctor told him that if he doesn't step down and retire, the stress is going to kill him. Since I'm the only one he trusts, I have to step in and take his place."

I sat down, stunned. "But what about us? What about our relationship? I suppose we can make a long distance relationship work, but I don't know. I don't know what I'll do without you."

With this he sighed. "I know."

We sat there in silence for a couple of seconds. Suddenly, he perked up. "I'll be back in a minute." He dashed into his bedroom and I could hear him rummaging around in his closet. He came back a few minutes later. He was holding something behind his back.

"Elise, I was waiting for Valentines Day to do this, but as you Americans say, there's no time like the present."

"What are you talking about?" I asked.

With that, he got down on one knee and presented a ring. It was a huge diamond solitaire. "This is what I really bought you in Antwerp. I was going to surprise you with it."

"Oh, I'm surprised, all right." I really was, too. The thing was big. And beautiful.

"Elise, would you be my wife? I was nothing without you and will be nothing again if you don't accept."

I didn't even have to think twice. "Of course," I said.

He smiled. "Thank you so much, Elise. I'll never disappoint you and I'm sure that you'll never disappoint me either."

I was still a little off balance. "But when? What about Antwerp?"

"You'll be coming with me, of course. That is, if you want to."

"But what about my job?"

He laughed. "So what about it? I'm rich. You don't have to work. Come to Antwerp and be a woman of leisure. We'll get married whenever. Your promise is enough for me at this point. We'll work out the details later."

I took a deep breath. A lot had happened today. I had shot a porno video, had sex with two strangers, gotten engaged, was moving to Europe and was now quitting my job. My head was spinning.

"Of course, you realize that we will have continue with this same arrangement as far as your sexuality goes," he said. "You'll have to commit to this or we will have nothing. Our relationship will be pointless. We will fail just like everyone else who is in a situation like ours. Are you ready for this step?"

I took a deep breath. He wanted this commitment. He wanted to continue to direct my sexuality.

"You have to promise me, Elise," he continued. "You have to trust me that I'll always have your best intentions at heart and that I'll only make you do the things that you desire but cannot bring yourself to do otherwise."

It was a big step. It was one thing to turn over your sexuality to a boyfriend, but to do it until death do you part was another thing entirely.

"Are you ready for this commitment? I have to know soon. I'll have to be in Antwerp next week."

I thought about it and how he had opened my eyes and my mind. How he had enriched my life. I thought about how hot he was and what Carolina had said about my sexuality and how precious a relationship like ours was. About how life was enjoyable only if you enjoyed yourself. This is what I had been doing and I knew that if I committed to him, I would continue to do so. He would have it no other way.

"Yes, I can commit. I submit to you completely. Whatever you want, I'll do. I trust you." I was sincere.

He smiled. "Good. Then let's make love."

20

And so that's how we left the United States.

We were on the plane to Antwerp. Of course, everyone was a little shocked and envious at the office when I told them I was quitting. They were even more envious when I told that I was moving to Europe.

I would miss Doreen, of course, along with some of the other girls, but it wasn't like I would never been seeing them again. I would be coming back to the States regularly to see family. Also Paul still had business there so my trips would probably be quite frequent.

Doreen had a big going away party for me. We invited everyone we knew. Even Ginger. It seems after our little tryst, Eric's true colors had come out even more vividly and she had decided that he really wasn't the guy for her. She could no longer overlook his faults. She just got sick of him. At first I felt a little badly for her, but she said that it was for the best. If he couldn't handle who she really was, she definitely couldn't stand who he really was either.

Of course, Paul and I had another threesome with her. I couldn't help but get wet just thinking about her. I couldn't resist putting my hand under my blanket and rubbing my clit just a little. This was one of the bonuses to going without panties. It was that much easier to masturbate. I liked Ginger and I was actually going to miss her. She was definitely the most sexually aggressive woman I had ever been with. I began to wonder if she could get enough time off to come to Belgium.

But enough of the fantasies, I was going to Europe.

I looked so forward to my new life. I looked forward to new friends and new experiences. I looked forward to the evolution of our relationship. I just knew that Paul was only getting warmed up and he would be providing me with more and more imaginative assignments. I knew that the sky was the limit and that my sexuality would only be enhanced by new surroundings.

I was okay with just him for now though. It would be a while before I would again feel the urge for more. Regardless, I knew it would only be a matter of time before I would get too horny to contain it. He would then come up with something more adventurous for me. I would do it and then everything would be okay until next time. I trusted him to help me take care of these needs.

As we flew, I thought more and more about our relationship and just how lucky I was. I not only had a very incredible man, I also had one who understood me. I had one who trusted me to love him even when I was fucking other people. I trusted him too. I would fuck anybody he told me too because I knew that he knew what I really wanted to do. If he had told me to fuck the pilots and the flight attendants right there in front of the passengers, I would have done it. I wouldn't have cared what anyone would have said about me either. This was me. Take or leave it. If anyone couldn't handle what I did or how I acted then that was their problem. Regardless of what happened, I would always submit to his whims because he knew what it took to satisfy me. Even better than myself. Carolina was so right. Sex with other people was so much more fun when you had someone you loved to go home to. When you didn't have to have all the self-doubt about the relationship-end of it and you were just free to concentrate on the sex. And when you could do it without hurting the one you love. So many women go through life feeling guilty for their sexuality. I was so fortunate that I had a man who could appreciate mine.

Paul looked over at me and smiled as we flew. I squeezed his hand. I was so happy.

It hit me just how liberating it was when you turn your sexuality over to someone else. I was doing whatever he wanted. I was doing whatever wild sexual fantasy popped in his head. It was such a turn-on to be in this position. To let go of inhibition and let someone else do the driving.

But who was I fooling. Seriously. Was I really doing whatever he wanted? No, not really. He was letting me do whatever *I* wanted. He was giving me the permission and the motivation to fulfill my lusts and fantasies. This was why I had never really protested about any of the extreme sexual stuff he had told me to do. It was because I had really wanted to do them. It was because I needed the adventure and the kink of being fucked by different people. It was indeed liberating to turn your sexuality over to someone else. But it was another thing entirely to give it to someone who understands you and knows what you want but are too afraid to do on your own. Paul had taken the pressure off me in regards to my inhibition. By allowing him to take charge, he was letting me run as free as I wanted. I remembered what Carolina had said about not having regrets. I knew that I would never regret what I was. A sexually insatiable woman.

So whatever he wanted. More like *whatever I wanted.* Life, finally, was good.

Other great fiction from New Tradition Books!

Playtime by Kim Corum. Have you ever wondered... What it would be like to have sex outside your relationship? What it would be like to have sex with your husband's best friend? Or, possibly, a woman? If you're like Mona, you don't have to wonder. You already know.

Eager to Please by Kim Corum. When Kara, the wife of a wealthy businessman, is kidnapped, the last thing she expects is to feel sympathy for her captor. As her time in confinement extends, she finds herself involved sexually and playing games of submission and dominance.

Now She's Gone by Kim Corum. Bruce doesn't know what happened to his wife, Sandy. All he knows is that she disappeared without a trace. Just when he's about to give up looking, he uncovers her journals which give him a closer look at her, her past, and her secrets.

Husband Swap and Roughing It: Two Dirty Stories by Kelly Carr. Two steamy erotic novels about frustrated wives who need some sex on the side. Women who crave other men so badly that they're willing to disrupt their comfortable lives just to realize their fantasies.

Male/Female/Male by Kelly Carr. A different kind of love story that's involves two good looking men and one hot woman. You figure it out.

Romantic Hedonism by Kelly Carr. What happens when a woman meets the man of her dreams in London? She prays her husband doesn't find out.

Slave Ship and Other Stories by Reggie Chesterfield. Featuring over-the-top tales of sexual adventure, this anthology is sure to please anyone who enjoys their hardcore erotica with a humorous twist.